The Stepsisters

The War
Between the Sisters

Tina Oaks

SCHOLASTIC INC.
New York Toronto London Auckland Sydney

ISBN 0-590-40902-6

12 11 10 9 8 7 6 5 4 3 2 1   7 8 9/8 0 1 2/9

Printed in the U.S.A.   01

First Scholastic printing, August 1987

The War
Between the Sisters

The Stepsisters

The War Between the Sisters
The Sister Trap
Bad Sisters

CHAPTER 1

Paige Whitman unzipped the plastic bag that held the dress she was to wear to her father's wedding. She had put off looking at the dress until the very last minute. When she learned the dress would be pink, she had groaned. There were colors she loved, colors she could take or leave alone, and then there was pink, which hated her as much as she hated it!

She lifted the bag out into the sunlight streaming through the hotel window and stared at the dress in horror. She had tried to prepare herself for pink, but she hadn't considered anything *this* pink. After all, pink could be anything from a pale shell color to a deep rosy tone. This was *pink* pink, bold and bright enough to make her eyes water.

And the style was as impossible for her as the color. She didn't even have to try the dress on to know how it would look. At sixteen she was taller

1

than most of her friends and thinner without being really skinny. But taller meant longer, and she knew her neck was too long to wear a low rounded neckline like that. And the sleeves! Her slender hands and long flexible fingers, which were wonderful for spanning the keyboard of a piano, always looked like bony sticks emerging from bracelet-length sleeves, even nice full ones like these.

Paige's instinct was to wail. Dresses were supposed to do things *for* you, not *to* you. The only tiny comforting thing she could think of was that Katie Summer Guthrie, her fifteen-year-old stepsister-to-be, would be wearing a matching monstrosity. Even though pink was a blonde's color, not even Katie could look like anything in *that* dress. It was comforting that she wouldn't be alone in her humiliation.

Beyond the other bed in the hotel room they shared, Paige's ten-year-old sister Megan hummed happily as she put on her own dress. Paige swallowed her groan. She had promised herself she wouldn't do or say anything to dampen Megan's high spirits.

Megan was a naturally happy-go-lucky girl, but Paige had never seen her as excited as she had been since their father announced his coming marriage to Virginia Mae Guthrie. Her father had tried to control his own excitement and tell them about his bride-to-be in a calm, sensible way. Paige knew him too well to be fooled, and anyway he gave himself dead away!

He started by telling them how he had met Virginia Mae on a business trip to Atlanta, then

2

how beautiful she was, and how gentle. He went from that to her divorce five years before and how she had been raising her three children alone ever since. Paige almost giggled. Here was William Whitman whose logic and cool courtroom delivery were legendary in Philadelphia legal circles. Yet he was jumping around from one subject to another as he talked about Virginia Mae.

"She's a writer," he said. "She does social and charity news for a paper down there. And that's not her only talent. Paige, wait until you hear her play the piano. She's wonderful."

They had all driven down to Atlanta earlier in the summer so the children could meet. It had been exciting. They had gone to Calloway Gardens where the water skiing championships were held and then picnicked on Stone Mountain. Paige had to agree that Virginia Mae Guthrie was as lovely as she was gentle. Although Megan had liked Mrs. Guthrie right away too, Megan had really lost her heart to the youngest Guthrie child, Mary Emily, who was Megan's own age.

Paige told herself that because she was older and more restrained than Megan, she had to know people better before she could make up her mind that firmly. But there was more to it than that. She had tried to shrug away the twinge of resentment that always came when she thought of Katie Summer. The girl *had* to be putting on an act. *Nobody* could possibly be as lighthearted and happy as she pretended to be, and nobody would be that pretty in a fair world. Seventeen-year-old Tucker seemed like a nice enough guy, although

3

his exaggerated good manners threw Paige off a little. Ten-year-old Mary Emily was cute. It was awkward being the only one holding back when her father and Megan were both so obviously deliriously happy.

Her father made the marriage plans sound so simple: "Right after our wedding, Virginia and the children will move up here to Philadelphia. We'll all be one big happy family together."

Paige had said nothing then or since, but concealing her doubts hadn't made them go away. She hated feeling like a sixteen-year-old grouch, but it just didn't make sense that everything would work out that easily. Not only would there be more than twice as many people in the same house as before, but the people themselves would be different.

Even if people from the South didn't *think* differently than people from the North, they certainly *sounded* different when they talked. And the Guthries were as completely southern as Paige's family was northern. Mrs. Guthrie and her three children had lived in Atlanta all their lives.

Paige slipped the dress over her head and fastened the zipper before daring to look into the mirror. She tried to smile back at her reflection but couldn't manage it. She had always secretly thought her long silky dark hair and the deep-set brown eyes she had inherited from her father were her best features. Even *they* did not survive the astonishment of the pink dress.

"How does it look?" Megan asked, coming around the end of the bed to join her.

When Paige turned, trying wildly to think of something truthful to say, she saw Megan's dress for the first time. "Megan!" she cried with honest delight. "You look fabulous!" She felt suddenly betrayed. How had the little girls had the good luck to get white dresses instead of pink? Then she realized, nobody would ever think of putting pink against Megan's dazzling red hair.

Megan's dress was a different matter altogether. Although the style was identical to Paige's dress, and Megan's wide belt was the same vicious shade of pink, it looked wonderful on her. Her reddish curls fell softly on her shoulders and the spatter of pale freckles she hated so much looked as if they had been painted there on purpose to give her a mischievous China doll look.

Megan giggled and fluffed out her full skirt. "Mary Emily's dress is just like mine. Isn't it great? I can't wait to show this dress back home."

Back home. Philadelphia meant only one person to Paige . . . Jake Carson. She shuddered at the thought of Jake seeing her in that pink dress. She would die, just simply die where she stood, if he ever saw her looking this gross.

She sighed and fiddled with the neck of the dress, wishing she hadn't even thought of Jake. Simply running his name through her mind was enough to sweep her with those familiar waves of almost physical pain. It didn't make sense that loving anyone could be so painful. But just the memory of his face, his intense expression, the

5

brooding darkness of his thoughtful eyes was enough to destroy her attempts to be sensible.

But even when Jake looked at her, he was absolutely blind to who she really was. She knew what he thought: that she was a nice kid, that she was fun to talk to, that she was William Whitman's daughter. Period. He didn't give the slightest indication that he even realized that she was a girl, much less a girl who loved him with such an aching passion that she couldn't meet his eyes for fear he might read her feelings there.

Then Megan was standing beside Paige, looking at both of them side-by-side in the mirror. Megan caught her lip between her teeth and frowned.

"Awful, isn't it?" Paige asked, smiling back at her sister's horrified reflection.

Megan looked pained and a little confused. "Not really awful," she began bravely. "Oh, Paige," Megan said miserably, still frowning as she studied her sister in the mirror, "is this going to be awful for you?"

Paige, who had been her father's right hand in a motherless household for most of her life, caught her younger sister in a quick hug. "Of course not!" she assured her. "How can a dress matter when what is happening is so important to all of us? And look at the good things. Dad's so happy he could pop. You and I get to have the fun of a *big* family. And a brother! Whoever thought we'd have a brother? Anyway, as you said, I only have to wear the dress this once."

Megan caught Paige around the waist and clung to her for a moment. "Sometimes I get scared,

6

thinking about the changes. It *is* going to be wonderful, isn't it, Paige?" Megan's voice held the first tremulous note of doubt Paige had heard from her sister.

"Absolutely wonderful," Paige assured her, wishing she felt as much confidence as she put into her tone.

Even as she spoke, she saw Jake's face again, his dark eyes intent on hers as he had talked to her about the wedding. "Look at your dad," Jake had said. "Anything that makes him that happy has to be a lucky break for all of you."

She had nodded, more conscious of how lucky she was to be with him than anything else. It was pure luck that their paths had ever crossed. She would never have met him if her father hadn't taken a special interest in Jake's ambition to become a lawyer, too.

Jake had done odd jobs at their house in Philadelphia for about a year and a half. She didn't believe in love at first sight, but it had almost been that way with her. From the first day, she found herself waiting breathlessly for the next time he came to work. She found herself remembering every word he had said to her, turning them over and over in her mind later. It wasn't that he was mysterious. It was more that she always had the sense of there being so much more in his mind than he was saying. She was curious about him, his life, his friends, how he thought about everything. In contrast to a lot of people who smiled easily and laughed or hummed when they worked, he was silent and withdrawn unless he was talking with someone.

Before he came, she hadn't realized how painful it was to love someone the way she did Jake. She hadn't asked to fall in love with him or anybody. She had even tried desperately to convince herself that he wasn't different from other boys, just nicer and older. That didn't work because it wasn't true. Jake really *was* different from the boys she knew at school. Although he talked when he had something to say, he was mostly a little aloof without being awkward and shy with it. And he wasn't an ordinary kind of handsome. His features were strong, with firm cheekbones, deeply set eyes, and a full serious mouth.

Maybe one day she would quit loving him as quickly as she had begun, but even thinking about that happening brought a quick thump of panic in her chest. Knowing how it felt to be so much in love, how could she bear to live without it?

"Dad's calling us," Megan said.

Startled, Paige snatched a last desperate glance at the mirror, groaned, and joined her sister at the door.

CHAPTER 2

When the wedding march began and the doors of the little chapel were opened, Paige was overwhelmed with the strange feeling that she was watching all this from a distance. Even as she walked beside Katie Summer and kept careful time to the music, a selection from Purcell that she loved, she didn't feel as if she was a part of what was happening.

The air in the high-vaulted room smelled sweetly fresh. The altar was decorated with regal pink and white gladiolas, just like the ones in the garden back in Philadelphia. Her father, tall, slender, smiling faintly, had never looked more distinguished or appealing than he did as he watched them walk toward him down the aisle.

Late morning sunlight angled from the high windows, touching Virginia Mae Guthrie's hair with sparkling lights. Pink ribbons from her bouquet swayed against the graceful folds of the skirt of her ivory dress. She walked serenely with her hand on her son Tuck's arm.

For no reason at all, Paige felt a sudden hot rush of tears behind her eyes. She had promised herself not to think about her own mother today, but the memory of the wedding picture in the family album shut away the scene before her eyes. Her mother had stood taller than Virginia Mae Guthrie. She had been candle slim in a glowing white dress; and her hair, as gloriously red as Megan's, had spilled out from under a crown of ivy leaves. Paige fought against her tears. She had been eight when her mother died, old enough to remember the silence in the house and her mother's scent lingering in the rooms. And her father's grief. That's what she had to keep remembering, her father's agonizing grief. The last thing her mother ever wanted was for her loved ones to be unhappy.

Paige felt a touch on her arm and looked over at Katie Summer at her side. Katie flashed her a quick sly smile that brought a fleeting dimple to her cheek. Paige swallowed hard, ducked her head, and looked away. Later she would have to deal with this girl, but not now, not while her father was repeating the same vows he had made so many years before to her own mother.

But that quick glance had been enough to remind her of how wrong she had been about how Katie Summer would look in her matching pink dress. It made Paige feel leggy and graceless beside her.

All the Guthries were good-looking. Tucker, at seventeen, was almost as tall as Paige's father, and comfortingly nice to look at in a curly brown-haired way. Mary Emily, behind with Megan, was button cute, with a grin that made Paige want to giggle. But the girl at Paige's side was just too much! Katie's thick dark blonde curls spilled in glorious profusion around her glowing face. *Her* pink dress picked up the rosiness of her deep tan and showed off the sparkle of her laughing blue eyes. Paige held her head high, fighting a sudden feeling of inadequacy that made her breath come short.

The beauty of the service finally made her forget herself. When the music swelled and she saw her father lean to kiss his new wife, she shut her eyes for a moment, repeating Jake's words over and over to herself.

"It'll be wonderful, just wait and see!"

Paige's father had said this would be a private family wedding. Paige didn't think much about that until the service was over and her father and his glowing wife turned to hug each of the children in turn. Paige looked into her step-mother's eyes and realized how thoughtful she had been. It would have been easy for this warm gracious woman to fill the chapel twice over with her friends. But she hadn't thought about her own pleasure. Instead, the only guest was her mother, Mrs. Summer, a sweet-faced woman with bright blue eyes and the same rich drawl that her daughter and grandchildren had. When Mrs.

Summer caught Paige with a hug, she whispered, "Welcome to my family, Paige, honey. You just can't know how I glory in having two fine new grandchildren!"

Paige grinned to herself, deciding that she gloried in being gloried in by Mrs. Summer.

Tuck drove them to his grandmother's house in Buckhead for brunch. With Mary Emily and Megan chattering beside her, Paige looked at the passing city with astonishment. How different Atlanta was from Philadelphia! The broad tree-shaded roads curved past handsome modern houses set back on deep lots. Bright flower beds contrasted sharply with the deep green of the giant pine trees that were everywhere. Why had she expected older houses with white columns like those in the pictures of the South?

Tuck caught her eye in the mirror and grinned. "Nothing like *Gone with the Wind,* is it?"

Paige felt herself flush. "How can you read my mind like that?"

Katie turned in the seat and laughed. "All yankees have that reaction to Atlanta. They forget *their* Union army burned this city to the ground."

Paige was glad to let that one alone, as Tuck turned into a circle drive to let them off at Grandma Summer's door.

Looking back, Paige was sure that the wedding brunch was as beautiful as any meal she would ever eat. The bridal colors of pink and white appeared again in the table linens and masses of flowers. Cold fruits were heaped on high pedestal dishes among trays of sliced meats and hot breads. The wedding cake served as a centerpiece.

During those hours, Paige found herself escaping again, pulling away from unexpected undercurrents of feeling that swirled around and in her.

Grandma Summer bent to Paige to make conversation, her soft voice rising in an exciting, different rhythm. "Virginia Mae tells me you play the piano, Paige, and that you're an excellent student. My, I know your father is just *so* proud of you."

Before Paige could reply she saw Katie's bright eyes watching and saw Katie's mouth pull down into a tight petulant expression. Paige was embarrassed. Mrs. Summer couldn't really care. She was only making polite conversation, but Katie's glance was enough to make Paige shy and awkward. "I play a little," Paige told Mrs. Summer. "I guess I've just been lucky at school. Mostly I like what I've taken so far."

Before her grandmother could respond, Katie ran her fingers through her glowing head of curls, turned away, and put her hand on Paige's father's arm. "I just had a perfectly *terrifying* thought," she said, looking up into his face. "My goodness, I hope you don't expect me to have a lot of talents or be a bookworm. I've got to tell you right off that I don't believe in all that."

After an astonished look, Paige's father covered Katie's hand with his and chuckled. "That's pretty interesting," he said. "What *do* you believe in, Katie Summer?"

Her laugh was quick and soft. "Having a *wonderful* time, just like I am today."

Naturally he beamed at her. Who could help it when everything she said sounded so intimate and appealing in that soft, coaxing drawl? Paige felt a shiver of icy jealousy. This was ridiculous! She wasn't jealous of her father's beautiful wife at all. In fact she was glad to see them exchange a loving glance. Her mother would have wanted him to be happy, too. But that Katie Summer was something else!

She caught herself sharply. This is only so difficult because we're all excited, she told herself. She made herself think about the upcoming drive to Philadelphia. Even though the trip would take a day and a half with an overnight at a motel, it would be fine because she would be too busy to worry about anything but the map. Her father had assigned her to navigate for Tuck Guthrie as he drove the kids all home in his mother's station wagon. Dad and Virginia Mae would follow with all the luggage his car would hold. Fortunately, most of the Guthrie things were already loaded on a moving van to arrive during the next week.

Oh, and the cat, Binker, would come in the station wagon, too. Paige winced at the thought of Katie and Mary Emily's fluffy white Persian cat sharing the same house with Scarlett, the Whitman's Irish setter. "One big happy family," her father had said.

She tried to force a bite of wedding cake past the funny hard lump in her throat. When we get back home to Philadelphia, everything will straighten out, she assured herself.

It simply had to!

After they all waved the bride and groom off, Katie Summer stood with her arm around her grandmother while Tuck loaded the luggage into the back of the station wagon. The two little girls had already piled into the back seat by the time Tuck closed the rear hatch, kissed his grandmother good-bye, and held open the front passenger door.

Katie Summer stared in disbelief as Paige serenely stepped past her and slid into the front seat.

"Hey," Katie said without thinking. "I *always* ride up there."

Paige looked up in amazement. "But I'm supposed to help Tuck navigate." She lifted the booklet from her lap. "I have the maps and everything."

"Maps work from the back seat, too," Katie protested. "Really, I always ride in the front seat, even when Mom is driving."

Before Katie could finish her sentence, Tuck was holding the rear door open, waiting. "Come on, Katie," he coaxed.

"I don't *want* to sit in back," she said firmly. "It's already crowded with those two kids and the cat carrier."

"Katie Summer," her grandmother protested, her voice gentle but firm. "Please don't make a fuss, dear."

Through this Paige had not even looked around, but stared straight ahead at the windshield as if she weren't at all involved in this ridiculous argument.

"Perhaps the three of you could ride up in

15

front," Grandma Summer suggested. "That would leave more room for the cat."

"Mom said somebody had to hold Binker's carrier all the way," Mary Emily said. "She gets hysterical."

"*I* may be hysterical if I have to ride back in that little space for a day and a half," Katie said, glaring at the back of Paige's neck.

"Maybe we can switch off later sometime," Tuck suggested, beginning to get annoyed. "Come on, Katie, climb in."

"Just for you," she told him softly. "And *just* for now."

Tuck fastened his seat belt and glanced around. "Everybody okay?" he asked warily.

"I'm fine," Paige said softly. Katie wanted to yank out that dark hair spilling over the back of the seat.

CHAPTER 3

Katie was still fuming inside when they finally reached the city limits of Atlanta. By the time they were an hour outside the city, she knew for certain she was never going to make it all the way to Philadelphia under these conditions.

She didn't mind carrying Binker's cat case on her lap. That was easier to handle than listening to the cat howl. But Mary Emily was playing some crazy game with Megan Whitman. Every time Katie relaxed even a little bit, the girls collapsed into giggles, Mary Emily fell against her, and Katie was thrown off balance.

She tried to ignore the girls by leaning forward to listen in on Tuck and Paige in the front seat. After only a minute of what she decided had to be the world's dullest conversation, she gave up on that. She could understand why Tuck was so interested in colleges, since he had only one year of high school left. But why in the world would even a stuffy selfish girl like Paige know that Philadelphia had forty colleges and universities in and around it?

Katie Summer not only didn't *know* how many colleges there were in Atlanta, she didn't care!

She plugged in her earphone radio and leaned back to listen to music. She had made a mistake back there. She shouldn't have made any fuss at all, but just gotten into the car. That way, when they climbed in the next time, she could have gotten there first and said it was her turn. She must have been more keyed up than she realized. She knew better than to make a fuss. When you smiled and kept things light, you *always* got your way in the end.

But at least the wedding *had* been wonderful.

The only thing that spoiled it at all was that stupid Paige Whitman. She had acted more as if it was a funeral than a wedding. What was the matter with that girl anyway? And why hadn't Katie herself seen this coming? Why hadn't she paid more attention to her own secret doubts about how great and exciting her new life was going to be?

But what a beautiful bride her mother had been, and what a handsome couple she and tall, dark William Whitman made. It was almost too romantic to bear! She had waited for this day with growing excitement all summer, thinking it marked the beginning of a whole new life for herself as well as her mother!

It still did, and she wasn't going to let that stick of a girl spoil it for her. She had been completely delighted when her mother decided to

18

marry again. She could think of nothing more thrilling than to move to a new place, meet new people, and be a part of a big, exciting city, and when she did feel any doubts, she had talked herself out of them. Never mind that northerners were supposed to be different. Kids were kids, and there had to be kids up north who enjoyed life as much as she did, even if they talked a little funny.

Then Paige had been such a wet blanket during the wedding. She had watched Paige from the corner of her eye. She both looked and acted strange. She was colder than Katie remembered from the visit the Whitmans had made earlier in the summer. And she hadn't looked nearly as good at the wedding as she had that day in jeans and a shirt. In fact, she had even managed to look like a stick in that wonderful pink dress Katie and her mother had ordered especially from Rich's department store. Not once had Katie seen Paige smile as if she really meant it. As for talking, when she did say anything, she was hardly a model of charm.

Katie settled the cat more firmly in her lap and yawned. The whole past month had been a whirl of fun. Three girl friends had thrown farewell parties for her, and when nothing else was planned, Eric had been there to take her to the swimming pool or out dancing. Would she miss Eric and her friends? Maybe a little bit, she admitted, but not much, and not for long. Philadelphia was a new world!

She wakened with a start, realizing that Paige

was leaning back from the front seat, whispering to the little girls. Katie pulled the radio earplugs out of her ears.

"You, Megan," Paige was saying, "scoot over a little closer to the window and give Mary Emily more room. You must have a quieter game, something that won't make you giggle so much."

"I'm all right," Katie mumbled sleepily. "I don't mind their noise."

"There's no reason for all that," Paige said. "Megan knows better."

Katie's eyes flew open. So Mary Emily *didn't* know better than to be noisy in a car? Who did this girl think she was, the great earth mother?

Apparently Megan thought so. Her voice dropped to a whisper, and Paige turned back in her seat again.

Katie stirred restlessly, feeling as if she had slept forever. But the silly August sun was still blazing in the western sky, and she was dying for a cold iced drink.

"How much longer until we get to have dinner?" Megan asked.

"You know better than to nag at the driver, Megan," Paige told her. "You know we promised to meet Dad in Ashville at a certain time."

Megan pulled back silently but Tuck grinned back over his shoulder. "We'll stop in less than an hour, Megan. We've already covered two hundred miles. Don't tell me you little kids are hungry already!"

"What do you mean 'already'?" Megan challenged him. "It's nearly six o'clock."

Tuck winked at Katie and turned back to

speak to Paige. "It sounds as if your little sister is as bad as ours . . . hungry all the time."

When Paige laughed and assured him that Megan could probably even out-eat Mary Emily, Katie shrugged. Maybe Paige would quit acting like a general reviewing her troops when she saw how diplomatically Tuck handled the little kids. And it was good to know that Paige knew *how* to laugh, even if it took somebody like Tuck to loosen her up. But everybody liked Tuck. How could they help it, when he was as handsome and charming as he was smart?

Twice more in that hour, Paige turned and bossed the little kids around. Katie was very tempted to lash out and ask if Paige thought Katie herself was behaving properly, but she held her tongue.

As promised, the newly married couple waited in the parking lot of the restaurant they had named. The food was served elegantly and was also delicious. The dining room featured a jazz trio that could play any song you wanted to hear. Katie hated to see the meal end because that meant getting back into that stupid car again!

She would have tried for the front seat but was embarrassed to start a scene with her mother watching. She crawled in the back and picked up Binker's cage, blazing with anger.

But at least feeding the younger girls made them both sleepy. When the conversation in the front seat turned from tedious to boring, Katie shut her own eyes and leaned back. By the time they finally stopped for the night, she had come up with this wonderful idea. She would enroll in

21

flight school the minute she was old enough to qualify. If she was lucky, she would never in her whole life have to take another trip by car!

The next morning, Tuck caught Katie before they reached the parking lot. "Come on, Katie," he said. "There's no point in starting this off on two left feet. You can live with the back seat one more day, can't you?"

"You know I can," she told him. "Now ask me what I intend to trade for it."

Either he didn't hear or didn't want to. In any case, he grinned and nudged her with his shoulder.

The second day of the trip was even worse! Katie was counting. The third time Paige turned around to scold the kids in the back seat, Katie spoke to her in the sweetest drawl she could manage. "Paige, wouldn't it be easier for you to run the back seat if you were *sitting* in it?"

She heard Paige's swift intake of breath but didn't care that she had shocked her. Paige stared at her coldly a minute, raised her eyebrows, and shrugged. "Apparently that doesn't work," she said. "At least not for you."

Katie was sputtering toward an answer when Tuck caught her eye with a pleading expression and she bit back her words. I'm keeping track, she told herself furiously.

By afternoon Katie had given up. She was too tired to care when Paige turned to boss the little girls. She was permanently deafened by Mary Emily and Megan's babbling and squealing in the seat beside her. When Binker expressed her discomfort in a plaintive howl, Katie almost joined in.

Then suddenly Mary Emily shouted in a different tone. "Look," she cried. "That billboard is advertising Philadelphia!"

From then on, the ride was fun. The city's spectacular skyline blazed with color against the night sky. Bridges and buildings along the river were outlined like Christmas trees, their lights shimmering in the moving water. Tuck concentrated hard on Paige's directions as he wound through the city traffic and up into the hilly residential district beyond.

With the city sparkling below them, Megan let out an excited cry. "There it is! That's our house right there!"

Katie stared at the Victorian house looming above them with astonishment. Although it was beautiful, it looked more like a picture in a book than a place people would really live. The house was tall and slender, painted a soft yellow with white shutters flanking its long, narrow windows. Fancy black iron designs trimmed the balconies and ran along the stairs that led down from the wide front porch. The hill was so steep that the front yard was several feet above the sidewalk. It was supported by a gray stone wall almost hidden under a tumble of blooming flowers.

Just as Tuck whistled a soft "Wow!" the front door opened. Katie's mother and Mr. Whitman stepped out into the gleam of the porch light to wave them into the brightly lit front hall.

CHAPTER 4

There was too much to see at once. Katie caught
a quick glimpse of a very formal living room on
her left with the dining room beyond. The walls
of the room to her right were covered with book
shelves behind a gleaming grand piano. Before
she saw any more, Tuck called to her from above.

He was standing halfway up a stairway that
curved from the hall to the second floor. "Come
on," he urged her. "I've got your luggage, but
you better bring Binker up to your room for the
time being." He grinned at her. "That's just in
case the Whitman dog figures out there's an
enemy in her territory."

As Katie gripped Binker's carrier, Mary Emily
and Megan ran up the stairs past Tuck to disappear behind the door of their own room down
the hall.

Paige was already waiting for Katie in the
room they were to share.

24

Katie looked around in horror. The room was very little larger than her own room in Atlanta. As if that weren't bad enough, the walls and woodwork were painted a shade of beige that had to be known as "Dusty Rat." Even with the lights on, it depressed Katie.

Paige had dumped her bag on the floor and was hanging her pink bride's maid dress in the back of a crowded closet. Paige's voice came muffled from the clothes. "I'll take the bed closest to the door because I get up early to walk the dog. I emptied out the top drawers in the bureau for you to use and gave you half the space in the closet. I hope it's enough."

Boss lady issues orders again, Katie told herself bitterly. She better not think she's going to whip me around like she does her little sister! And enough space? The whole room was enough to send her screaming out into the street again! Paige had to be kidding! Only one closet for the two of them? Only that stretch of beige rug between her and Miss Poker Face of the Western World? And what about drawers? A single tall dresser stood against one wall with a small round mirror over it.

I hate it, Katie told herself. I hate this room. I hate this place. I hate the stiff way she's standing there, knowing I hate it and just glorying inside to see me miserable. I won't share this room with her, that's all. When Mom sees this, she'll figure out something. But with the thought came the memory of her mother's voice. "We'll all have adjustments, Katie. You'll share a room."

Paige was at the door, still watching her. "Dad

said we should just drop our things and go downstairs. Apparently Miss Aggie left a surprise for us in the kitchen."

"Miss Aggie?" Katie asked. This was a name she hadn't heard before.

"Our housekeeper." Paige explained. "She's kept house for Dad and Megan and me ever since our mother died."

"Does she live in?"

Paige shook her head. "Oh no. She lives with her daughter across town and comes in every day. She must have made a special trip over today because Sunday is her day off."

Katie, still holding the cat carrier, nodded. "Tell your father I'll be right along. I want to settle Binker down a little."

Katie took Binker out of her carrying case and held her on her shoulder, as she stared around thoughtfully. After a moment, she crossed the room and very quietly opened the empty dresser drawers, trying to picture what she could put into them. There wasn't room for anything more than her underwear and panty hose. This was *impossible*! How could anyone think two girls could exist in this dark cave?

The only halfway decent thing about the place was a row of tall windows between the twin beds. The windows opened out on a narrow balcony that looked down on the street. Beyond, the city glittered with thousands of sparkling colored lights.

It was a matter of both pride and habit that Katie Summer never cried from hopelessness. There was always some way to handle a bad situation. But now she couldn't think of anything in the world that would help what she had gotten into with Paige Whitman. She held Binker close, feeling hot tears matting the silky white fur. "It can't end like this," she whispered against Binker's warm neck. "All those wonderful dreams can't possibly end like this."

Over the cat's purring, Katie heard other sounds. Her mother's laughter rose softly from downstairs, and she recognized Tuck's touch on the piano, playing a pop version of the wedding march.

Katie shook her tears away, closed the door, locking Binker inside, and stood in the hall a moment, taking one deep, painful breath after another, until she had control of herself.

"Okay, new life, here I come!" she whispered, then forced herself to run lightly down the stairs.

The moment Paige wakened she was conscious of her new stepsister there in her room. It was weird to wake up in your own room with an almost absolute stranger. Paige frowned and listened. What was even more weird was what she heard, a soft rhythmic rumbling.

She listened a moment in confusion. The sound wasn't as threatening as it was just strange. She rose on one elbow to look over toward the other twin bed across the room. Katie Summer slept quietly with one golden tanned leg on the outside of her covers, and her face completely hidden by the tumbled mass of her curls.

Paige realized at once where the sound was coming from. In the middle of Katie's pillow, just above her head, the white cat Binker sat watching Paige. The cat had folded her front legs in under her chest to make a perfect ball of herself. She stared with unblinking eyes at Paige, purring more loudly than any cat Paige had ever heard.

Paige slid silently out of bed and went to the closet. The cat yawned, stretched, and followed her, looking up with curious blue eyes. Paige put her jeans and shirt over her arm and looked at Binker. It seemed rude not to stroke her when she was being so attentive. Binker's purr increased in volume at Paige's touch and her back rose to Paige's hand, as if she had been waiting all night for just that petting.

Unfortunately, Paige was through before the cat was. As she started for the door, the cat ran swiftly behind her, still looking up eagerly.

Finally, by pushing the cat's face back forcibly, Paige escaped to the bathroom with a sigh of relief.

"Day one of the rest of my life," she told herself as she adjusted the shower faucets and gingerly tested the spray with a single foot. She remembered all the reasoning she had gone through when her father first told her she would have to share a room with her new stepsister.

The world is full of girls who *never* had a room of their own, she had told herself.

If all those other girls can manage it, I surely can, she had told herself.

But she hadn't met Katie Summer Guthrie then. There were probably a hundred thousand girls in the world she could share a room with comfortably. She doubted that Katie was among their number.

But the cat was pretty. She couldn't remember ever seeing a prettier cat. But then, she couldn't remember seeing many girls as pretty as Katie Summer. Would Katie's flirting and brightness bother her so much if the girl were dull or colorless?

On second thought, she didn't want to answer that question.

Instead, she should ask herself how she would feel in a strange town, a strange house, sharing a room with a strange stepsister.

Not great. But she wouldn't look around the room with that superior look on her face and practically sniff at everything she saw, either.

Day one, she told herself again. Whatever that means! After brushing her teeth and towel-drying her long dark hair, she realized her wire brush was still in her suitcase in the bedroom. She fished in the bathroom closet but only found a fine-toothed comb that wouldn't last two seconds in her hair. She shook her hair, combed it with her fingers, and tiptoed down the stairs.

If she was lucky, Jake would get to the Whitman house for the day just about when she got back from running the dog. After the painful days just past, she was so eager to see him that it didn't even matter that she would ache in that painful way when he looked at her. It would be wonderful just to talk to him. He would be interested in the wedding. Not that she would dare complain about the pink dress or how awkward she had felt. Just seeing him would make everything upsetting that had happened seem very much behind her.

She would feel at home again.

Even though it was too early for Miss Aggie to be there, the downstairs hall smelled richly of coffee. Paige pushed open the swinging door and saw her father and Virginia Mae in the sunny kitchen alcove. They looked like a coffee commercial, her father in his deep blue robe and Virginia Mae radiant in a silk kimono, the color of an apricot. They smiled up at her over their coffee cups.

"Look who's bright and shiny!" Virginia Mae said, reaching for Paige's hand.

"She's always been an early bird," Paige's father said, pulling her down for a quick kiss on the cheek.

Paige caught her breath. Ever since the wedding was announced she had wondered what she should call Virginia Mae. Her father had given her the perfect opening to ask. "It looks like you have two early birds now, Dad. What do I call the other one?"

Virginia Mae laughed softly. "What a diplomat! But I admit I've wondered about that, too. Personally I don't care, as long as you're comfortable with what you settle on. Do you have any ideas, Bill?"

He shook his head. "If I know you, Paige, you'll do the deciding for yourself in the end. Megan has made her decision. She fell right into calling Virginia 'Mom' because Mary Emily does."

Paige tested the word in her mind as she poured herself orange juice. She drank it slowly, set the empty glass on the counter, and grinned over at both of them. "Now the following is a test. Listen carefully and see if it sounds like an emergency! I'm going to take Scarlett down to the park for a run, *Mom*. When Miss Aggie comes, tell her I'd love two eggs scrambled and hash browns." She grinned wickedly. "Hey, not bad!"

Paige was startled to realize that Virginia Mae was too touched to reply.

The big Irish setter hurled herself against the sides of the dog house when she saw Paige come out the back door. She whimpered with happiness and leaped to swipe Paige's face with a welcoming tongue as Paige snapped the lead onto her collar.

"Run, Scarlett," she whispered. "Let's go! We need to time ourselves to get back when Jake arrives!"

"Mom," Paige repeated aloud softly as she raced down the hill, trying to keep up with the Irish setter. The name felt right, and just saying it made her feel warm.

Maybe Katie would settle down and stop acting as if the world belonged to her. Maybe Katie could even get used to the fact that Paige had some rights, too. It was funny that just knowing that Jake would be there when she got back from the park made everything look more hopeful.

Sometimes she wondered if hearts ever really burst right inside a person's chest.

CHAPTER 5

Katie Summer groaned and tried to bury her head in the pillow as Mary Emily and Megan thundered down the hall, racing each other to the top of the stairs. Binker mewed softly and tapped Katie's cheek with her paw.

"I'm not ready," Katie protested, pushing the cat away. As she did, she saw the sheets of Paige's empty unmade bed spilling onto the floor.

Katie sat up swiftly. "Oh my gosh. I clean forgot. I am in Philadelphia!" When she looked around the room she groaned again. If anything, the room looked even worse in daylight. Not only were the walls and rug still a dreadful color, but Paige's suitcase still yawned in the middle of the floor next to her unmade bed.

Escaping Binker, Katie showered and rushed back for her clothes. After pulling on a pair of pink shorts with a matching T-shirt, she looked around for a full length mirror.

"This is ridiculous," she told Binker. "That silly little round one above the dresser is the only mirror in this room." She made a mental note to mention this to her mother the first chance she got.

Since the dresser mirror was of no use, she walked out onto the balcony as she brushed her hair. The city seemed to stretch forever beyond the wooded park across the street. She saw the corner of a parking lot in the park and little walking paths that led back and forth into the trees. Nice! Chimneys poked through green foliage and she heard the distant hum of traffic. But there was a closer sound, something like a motor choking somewhere below. The sound died, began again, and then pulsed with a steady rhythm. She leaned over the balcony rail and looked at the lawn below.

At first she saw nothing but one clipped line of grass looking paler than the rest of the lawn. Then as she watched, a young man pushing the lawn mower came into view. She stared in disbelief. This couldn't be happening. A girl just didn't look out the window of her new home and see the best-looking boy she could imagine, walking back and forth in her own front yard. She studied the lines of his suntanned back. He was big and solid without having an ounce of fat anywhere. His hair was a dark, rich brown that caught lights from the sun. She waited for him to turn, fully prepared for him to be miserably ugly.

As he turned to approach, he glanced up. For a long moment their eyes met. Katie Summer didn't even have the presence of mind to smile

33

at him. She simply looked at him, feeling that somehow this was the most important moment of her life. His eyes were shadowed by his lashes, but his mouth, as unsmiling as her own, parted as if he had something to say but lacked the words. Katie gripped the edge of the balcony railing, suddenly giddy. She had liked a lot of boys, including Eric, of course. She had seen a lot of boys that looked promising. She had never looked into a boy's face and felt her world unsteady under her feet.

As they stared at each other, the lawn mower coughed and went out. His face darkened, and he lifted both hands in a swift gesture, as if to say, "Why fight it?" Then he smiled before he knelt to start the motor again.

Katie backed into the room and caught her breath. Why did he make her think of all the most romantic men in the world, only much improved? He slightly resembled Rhett Butler, only younger and with no mustache. Maybe he was more like Heathcliff in *Wuthering Heights*, without the angry eyebrows. She was thinking about James Dean being a brunette when she recovered her senses.

"I can't be feeling this way about a guy I don't know," she told Binker. "I'll go down and meet him and get myself under control. If he works here, I have a perfect right to get to know him!"

At the door she paused, frowned a moment, then went back to change her clothes, putting on her best white shorts and a boat-necked shirt that matched her eyes.

34

Katie Summer followed her nose into the fragrant kitchen. The table in the breakfast alcove was filled with family. She barely glanced at them before walking swiftly over to the gray haired woman by the stove. The woman looked astonished as Katie seized her hand and smiled winningly at her.

"*You* must be Miss Aggie," Katie said warmly. "I'm just *that* excited to meet you. The sandwiches you made for us last night were absolutely fabulous. That was the most *thoughtful* thing I've ever heard of."

"Thank you," Miss Aggie said, pulling back a little to look at Katie. Then she smiled. "I'm just glad you liked them. It was my pleasure to help welcome you all home."

Katie would have been off again except that Tuck spoke firmly. "Down, Katie," he said. "All the way down! Sit!"

Katie grinned at Tuck, stuck out her tongue, and took a chair. When she glanced around the table, she looked surprised. "Where's Paige?" she asked. "She was gone when I woke up."

"Walking Scarlett," Mr. Whitman replied. "She should be back any minute."

"Scarlett?" Katie repeated.

Tuck laughed. "That gave me a little shock, too," he told her. "Scarlett is the dog . . . an Irish setter."

When Katie continued to stare, her mother laughed. "Scarlett O'Hara is a *very* Irish name."

"I caught a glimpse of Paige and the dog leaving," Tuck said. "That is a beautiful dog, but she sure gives Paige a run for her money."

As he spoke Paige came in the back door, her cheeks glowing from the run and her uncombed hair a tangle from the wind. "Come have some breakfast," her father said. "You must have given Scarlett a real workout."

Paige caught a deep breath. "Actually it was the other way around. She was punishing me for being away, I guess. I thought I was going to have to drag her up the hill to get her back home."

Tuck had risen when she entered. He pulled out her chair and waited there until she sat down.

Paige grinned at him, finding it hard to believe a boy could be that polite. Was he for real?

Mr. Whitman said with a smile. "Katie, would you like to pass the muffins to Paige?"

Katie held out the plate to Paige. "You left the room too early to see the real show," she told her.

"Show?" Paige asked, confused.

Katie sparkled and shrugged her shoulders. "I *like* Philadelphia! I woke up to see a gorgeous hunk of man in my very own front yard."

"Katie!" her mother rebuked her. "What a thing to say!"

"It's only the truth, Mom," Katie said, spreading raspberry jam on her muffin. "Aren't you always telling me that a *real* lady tells the truth?"

"That's different from calling it exactly like you see it, or him, Katie," her brother said. He always found Katie's outspokenness surprising. Southern ladies were supposed to be more discreet, and southern gentlemen were supposed to

36

be . . . gentlemen. Tuck acted the role, even though he sometimes found it pretty tough going.

"Jake," Megan said suddenly, as is she had just figured it out. "She's talking about Jake Carson. He works here, and he's really a super guy. He put up my swing."

"Jake! Of course," Mr. Whitman said and then laughed. "He would die if he heard you call him a hunk. He's a brilliant kid, he'll make an outstanding lawyer one day."

"And he works here?" Katie's mother asked.

Katie heard Mr. Whitman launch into a long explanation of how impressed he had been with Jake Carson from the first time he met him. "He comes from an old Philadelphia family which has produced some of the finest leaders the city has had."

"But he still does yard work?" Virginia asked in a puzzled voice.

Mr. Whitman laughed. "You forget the old yankee ethic is still alive and thriving in Philadelphia. He graduated from high school last year, but decided to take a year off before starting into the long grind of college and law school. He lives at home but pays his way and earns his own spending money. When he approached me about this job, I couldn't believe my own good luck. He's a great boy, as well as the kind of person we need in the legal profession."

Katie tuned the conversation out. Who had time for that? Jake Carson could be getting ready to leave. She took the last bite of her muffin, wiped her hands, and rose.

"Where are you going, Katie? You haven't been excused." Her mother's voice was disapproving.

Katie sighed and stood with her hands on the back of the chair. Her tone was coaxing. "Don't be a fuddy-duddy, Mom. May I please be excused? I only want to meet this great Jake."

"What about Eric?" Mary Emily asked.

Tuck laughed as Katie felt her cheeks redden. Did her family *have* to run her business in front of everyone? "*Eric* is in Atlanta," Katie said coldly. "*I'm* here."

"If you can wait just a minute, I have a question," Mr. Whitman said. "I want to know how the room is going to work. Do you need anything?"

Katie groaned inwardly. Did he have to ask when she didn't have half a minute to spare? "There are problems," she said as lightly as she could. "The most pressing one is that we have no full-length mirror!" She drew her hand across the line of her shoulders and smiled at him as winningly as she knew how. "Would you believe, I feel like the bust of Brahms in the music room?" She turned to her mother. "Excused, Mom?"

Her mother sighed but did not meet her eyes. "You are excused, Katie Summer." Her voice trailed off.

A wave of actual nausea had gripped Paige at Katie's first comment about the "hunk of man." Unlike Megan, she didn't have to figure out who Katie was referring to. The painful thud in her

38

stomach told her it was Jake who had made Katie's eyes sparkle like that and sent her rushing away from the table with her breakfast half eaten.

Katie and Jake. Jake and Katie. She should have seen it coming. She fought to hold back a sudden rush of tears as she watched Katie's slender figure disappear beyond the swinging hall door.

It was unbelievable that only a few moments earlier she had thought it was dreadful that she had only had a chance to wave at Jake as she dragged Scarlett back home. That was nothing compared to this.

Tuck's voice seemed to come from a long way off. "Are you okay, Paige?"

"You really do look a little sickly all of a sudden," her father told Paige with concern in his voice.

"Maybe Scarlett was too hard for her to drag up that hill," Mary Emily suggested.

Paige stiffened and forced a reassuring smile. "I'm okay," she said. "I was just dizzy there for a minute."

"Maybe you should lie down and let it go away," Mary Emily said. "That's what Mom makes me do."

Lie down and let it go away. The words echoed in Paige's mind, and she fought the tears again. Whether she lay down or stood up to fight wouldn't make any difference. What was breaking her heart was not going to go away because of anything she did!

CHAPTER 6

Katie Summer opened the front door and quietly let herself out onto the porch. The air was rich with the combined scents of freshly mowed grass and the petunias blooming beside the steps. The lawn mower pulsed from the far end of the yard, almost drowning out the chirping of the birds in the hedges. Two delicately carved pillars flanked the stairs leading down to the front walk. Katie crossed the porch and leaned lightly against one of the pillars to wait for Jake to come closer.

It was ridiculous for her heart to hammer like this! You would think she had never seen a good-looking young man before. But she hadn't really . . . not *that* good-looking. She had a wild moment of doubt. Were her shorts pressed? Would she look more casual and natural if she had put on nicely fitted jeans? It was too late to worry about that now. The throbbing of the motor swelled steadily as Jake approached the front sidewalk. He guided the machine with his head down, carefully overlapping the last swath of grass he had cut. When he reached the flower bed he glanced up and saw Katie.

She had meant to smile the minute he looked up, but somehow she wasn't able to. She could only stare back at him, as if she were hypnotized. He stood very still as the motor coughed a couple of times, then died. He didn't even seem to hear it, but only kept staring at her, not saying anything, not moving a muscle.

His eyes were unbelievably dark, their color shadowed by his lashes. His expression in that moment of surprise at seeing her was strangely disturbed, making her want to run to him and comfort him. Her feelings didn't make any sense. Finally she caught her breath and managed to smile at him.

That broke the spell. A wonderful wide grin swept his face and he laughed as if he were laughing at himself. He left the mower and walked to the foot of the steps, where he stood looking up at her and smiling.

"Well," he said, his tone still warm with laughter. "I've heard of the face that launched a thousand ships, now I am seeing one that will choke up a gasoline motor. You have to be Katie Summer. I'm Jake Carson." As he spoke, he wiped his right hand on the back of his jeans and offered it to her.

His hand felt moist and cool and strong in hers. "You guessed right," she said, wishing her voice was not quite so whispery. "I'm very glad to meet you. Mr. Whitman . . . Dad . . . says wonderful things about you."

He released her hand but stood looking at her intently. The expression in his dark eyes was somehow unreadable. How frustrating! Whenever she *wanted* to blush, she never could. Now that she particularly *didn't* want to, she felt the color rush into her cheeks.

"So you're here. Welcome to Philadelphia," he said, still not looking away. "What do you think of it?"

"It was beautiful when we came in last night," she said, meaning to add that she hadn't really seen the city at all.

He laughed softly. "It is even more beautiful this morning."

Katie wondered how should she deal with this? The boys back in Atlanta had always made very direct compliments, things she could respond to with a simple "Thank you." What Jake said had *sounded* like a compliment without being anything she could respond to.

He tilted his head and studied her. "Is your little sister as different from Megan as you are from Paige?"

"I . . . I don't think so," she stammered. Maybe Megan and Mary Emily looked different, but no two girls in the world could possibly be as different from each other as she and Paige were.

"She's a good friend," he said, finally releasing her hand. "All the Whitmans are good friends." He grinned. "But if I want to keep coming around here working for them, I better get that thing

42

going again." He started away, then turned back. "Katie Summer, I hope I see a lot more of you."

"I would like that very much," she said softly.

He looked startled and she was suddenly embarrassed. Her mother's lectures about being a real southern lady echoed in her mind. Had she been too honest? As she made a quick escape into the house, she could feel his dark eyes following her until the door was shut behind her.

Katie Summer found the breakfast table clear except for coffee cups in front of her mother and Mr. Whitman.

"There you are, Katie," he said. "I hope you won't mind that we went ahead and made plans without you. We've figured out a quick bike tour of Philadelphia. Maybe it will help you feel more at home when school starts. That's okay, isn't it?"

"Okay?" she echoed. Then she grinned at him. "It's glorious!" Jake's words were still echoing in her head, "I hope I see a lot more of you." Until she saw him again she didn't give a hoot what happened. "Glorious!" she repeated, ignoring her mother's startled look.

Paige only half heard the discussion about the day's plans. Her mind had gone down the hall and out onto the porch with Katie Summer. Even through the closed front door she heard the lawn mower stop and knew in her heart what was going on.

Jake had stopped working as he always did when she went out to talk to him. He would be standing there looking at Katie intently, the way he had looked at *her* so many times before. But what he was seeing was too much of a contrast. Paige felt herself shrivel inside. It wasn't fair that Katie was so glowing and alive with her fair hair and shining blue eyes. Of course Jake would be overwhelmed by her, the way Paige herself had been the first time she saw her. He was human, wasn't he? And why would he ever again look at anyone as dull and dark and awkward and plain as herself?

The minutes dragged on. Her bite of muffin stuck painfully halfway down her chest. When Tuck got up to put the bike carrier on the station wagon, Paige rose too.

"I'll help him, Dad," she said. "It's always easier with two."

Virginia Mae smiled. "What a great team we have going here," she said. "Isn't that pretty heavy work, Paige?"

"Listen," her father said. "That lady is my right hand. There isn't much in this world she can't do."

Tuck's gallantry startled Paige at every turn. He held the door and then closed it behind them. "It must be great to have your dad so proud of you," he said with a wistful tone in his voice.

"He's prejudiced," Paige told him. Scarlett had begun barking wildly the minute they got outside.

"What a dog!" Tuck said. "Want to wait here until I get the stuff together?"

Paige nodded and went to stroke Scarlett. She needed a moment to get control of her angry sense of loss anyway. While Tuck backed the wagon from the garage and got down the bike carrier, she held Scarlett's head between her hands and fought back tears. Her father was more than prejudiced, he was dead wrong.

"Want a list of the things I can't do, Scarlett?" Paige asked bitterly. "I can't make Jake see I feel like more than a friend. Now I can't bear to see him enchanted by a fickle, empty-headed girl like Katie. It isn't fair."

Scarlett, catching the feeling behind her words, whined softly. As Tuck brought the bike carrier out of the garage, Megan and Mary Emily exploded from the back door, took the steps two at a time, and raced each other toward the garage.

"The giggling horde is closing in," Tuck called to Paige.

With Scarlett barking and leaping with excitement, they loaded the bikes and fastened them into place. As they finished the last one, Paige's father and Virginia appeared at the back door.

"Everybody ready?" Mr. Whitman called. "Where's Katie?"

"Dreaming in the bathroom mirror," Mary Emily said, grabbing Megan's hand. "We'll get her down."

Dreaming, Paige's mind echoed. Dreaming about Jake already?

Katie was astonished by Fairmount Park. She had thought the parks in Atlanta were beautiful, especially the one around the mansion where the president of Emory University lived. The lake there, busy with wild ducks and geese, had seemed magical with its miniature house tucked on a tiny island. But this park was incredible!

They passed the Art Museum and followed a

bike path toward the Schuykill River. The park not only seemed to stretch for miles but there were people everywhere. They wheeled past a rugby game, past baseball diamonds, and soccer games.

When they reached the river, Katie slid off her bike to stare. Sail boats with colorful spinnakers dotted the water's surface as far as she could see. In among them, rowers were speeding their craft with rhythmic oars, the sun gleaming on the rowers' tanned arms. "Awesome!" she breathed out loud to herself.

The family had gone on up the path beyond her. Tuck turned around to shout back at her. "Come on, Katie," he called. "Catch up!"

"I'm coming," she replied without moving. What good athletes the rowers were. Suddenly all the familiar sports looked awkward, basketball jumpy, football rough and lumpy. "Awesome!" she breathed again and picked out a single boat to keep pace with as it sped downstream.

She took the trail closest to the river, passing joggers and hikers and spinning past clusters of people picnicking in the grass. All around the park were small formal gardens with statues in unexpected places.

And this fabulous park was in Jake's city. Maybe he would bring her here sometime. She shaded her eyes with her hands as the boat she had been racing with drew ahead and disappeared among a cluster of sailboats. Jake will bring me here, she promised herself. I'll see to that.

CHAPTER 7

Paige decided that Tuck had to be the best company in the world on a bike trail. He was not only a steady rider but his enthusiasm was catching. She found herself laughing at his comments as they rode along. The younger girls were up ahead with Paige's dad and Virginia following.

Although Tuck kept seeing new things that interested him, she noticed that now and then he looked back down the path with expectation and something else . . . annoyance.

"How do you like our park?" Paige's dad called back.

"It's super, sir," he said. He never forgot that "sir." It was what he had been taught.

"We come a lot," Mr. Whitman told him. "The girls and I love the zoo. It's the oldest one in the country."

"And the theater," Megan added. "And the horseback riding."

47

"Horseback riding," Mary Emily cried. "Oh, can we?" She wheeled around to ride back by her mother's side. "They have horses to ride, Mom. Can we? Katie loves horses as much as Megan and I do."

Her mother nodded, then frowned, looking around. "Where *is* Katie?"

"She stayed back to watch the rowers," Tuck told her. "I told her to catch up and she said she would."

Paige's father stopped, shaded his eyes, and looked back along the path. "Maybe I better go look for her."

"I'll go back for her, sir," Tuck offered, irritated with Katie for holding everybody up.

Paige's father shook his head. "You stay here with the girls and your mother. It's my turn to try."

After he left, the rest of them wheeled onto the grass to wait. Virginia Mae sat on a shaded bench while Tuck and the girls and Paige sprawled in the grass.

"The horseback riding," Mary Emily reminded her mother.

"Not this trip. We have too full a day. We'll catch a sandwich here, then go home and change for shopping and dinner."

"Soon, then," both girls pleaded.

Virginia Mae laughed and reached down to brush the hair off Megan's forehead. "Patience, you two. We have all the rest of our lives, remember?"

The words threw the girls into giggling, which ended with a roll on the grass and a contest to see who could turn the most cartwheels before collapsing with exhaustion.

Virginia's words made Paige wince. What good was the rest of your life if it was as miserable as the last two days had been? Could she really get used to sharing her father? To having Katie and her cat there in her own private space? She didn't dare even let herself think about Jake.

Virginia Mae didn't say anything, but Paige saw her look at her watch several times. They had waited a long time without any sign of her father and Katie. Tuck offered again to go look for them, but his mother just shook her head.

The girls settled into whispering in the grass, and Paige leaned against a tree with her eyes shut. Katie couldn't be lost forever no matter how nice that sounded.

When Mary Emily yelled and Virginia rose, Paige knew her father and Katie were back. Katie's bright melodious voice grated on her ears.

"I'm really sorry, Mom," Katie said gaily. "I just got completely carried away watching those rowers. You do forgive me?"

Paige opened her eyes to see Katie gripping her father's arm and smiling up into his face, just as she had imagined her smiling up at Jake.

She would have shut her eyes again but Tuck was leaning over, offering her his hand. "Wake up, sleeping beauty," he told her. "It's lunch time."

Nobody pointed out that they were off schedule because of Katie Summer. Instead, Katie walked her bike between the parents all the way back to the lunch stand, steadily chattering on about how beautiful the rowers were and how she couldn't wait to see them again.

All the rest of my life, Paige reminded herself miserably.

By the end of that afternoon, Paige felt as if she had *already* lived a lifetime. She didn't mean to keep track, but she couldn't help adding up the things about that day that were impossible.

Lunch was barely all right, as was the trip back home along the wide avenue that led from the park. The trouble started again when they got home.

"If you don't mind, I'll shower first," Katie Summer said, with her fresh outfit already neatly folded over her arm. "You haven't made your bed anyway and I'll hurry."

Paige stared after her, then looked around the room. All the mess in the entire room was her own. "How could I make my bed and help Tuck with the bikes at the same time?" she muttered angrily. It didn't work. She knew she wouldn't have made her bed anyway. Certainly she wouldn't have done it like Katie had, with the bedspread drawn so neatly over the blankets. Katie's cat had curled in Paige's untidy sheets. Binker stared back without stirring when Paige tried to call her off.

"Okay, Binker," Paige said, scooping her up and dropping her right in the middle of Katie's carefully smoothed bed.

Paige frowned as she looked into her closet a long time before picking out a navy linen skirt and white blazer that she thought would work both for shopping and dinner downtown. Her panty hose were wadded up on the closet floor, but at least they hadn't run. When she was all ready to take her shower, and Katie was still in the bathroom, she gave up and made her bed.

The hands on her alarm clock scared her. She heard the little girls pound down the stairs and soon after that, her father's voice calling. "You girls almost ready?"

"Katie is still in the bathroom," Paige called down.

"Maybe you could use the other one," he suggested after a minute. "We really *are* running late."

"But my things are in there," Paige wailed. "My shampoo."

"Please, Paige," he said quietly. "Let's not make a fuss."

Paige had never showered so fast nor felt worse afterward. Megan's shampoo smelled like pine needles and didn't leave her hair shiny. When she came out and started into her own bathroom for the hair dryer, her father called upstairs that everyone was waiting.

"But I have to dry my hair!" Paige wailed again.

"It's a warm day, honey," he coaxed. "Can't you just come on and let us get started?"

Paige shivered as she stood in the door with her robe over her arm. The cat was back on her bed. She dumped the robe on the floor, tossed the cat over on Katie's bed, and wished she had never been born.

Everyone in the car was very quiet during the

ride downtown. Katie and her mother had apparently had an argument about clothes because Katie was not wearing the outfit she had taken to the bathroom. She *had*, however, put on every chemical known to woman. Crowded in the back seat between the little girls, Paige had a fit of sneezing.

"Catching a cold?" Megan asked.

Tuck either guessed the truth or was having trouble breathing, too. "Air pollution," he told Megan. "Otherwise known as Katie Summer's perfume collection."

Katie looked daggers at her brother as Paige swallowed a giggle.

Every kind of mirror in the world was on display in an alcove at the end of the furniture department at Wanamaker's. After dragging Katie almost bodily past several displays of the latest clothes, they picked out two door mirrors, full length, one for Katie and Paige's room and one for the little girls.

Paige drifted around looking at furniture, while her father and Virginia paid for the mirrors and made arrangements for their delivery. As Paige passed the mirror display again, she saw Katie preening in a three-way mirror, wholly absorbed in herself and what she had on. Paige went on silently to where Tuck was examining a wall of grandfather clocks. Then the parents were ready to go and no one could find Katie . . . again.

"She's down there," Paige said, pointing to the alcove at the end. She followed as they walked along, mean enough to hope Katie was still entranced by her own image. For once she got her wish.

Katie was turning from side to side, admiring the back of her full skirt and making what she thought were sophisticated faces. When Tuck chuckled softly, she looked up to see the entire family watching her, trying not to laugh at her. She straightened, blushed deeply, and smoothed her skirt.

"Come on, Katie," he mother said, obviously annoyed. "We've looked all over for you. You've kept us all waiting."

"We never would have found you if Paige hadn't known where you were," Mary Emily said brightly.

"*I* should have guessed," Tucker said.

Paige wondered if Tuck was used to angry looks like the one Katie gave them both. He must have been because he only shrugged, grinned at her, and started for the escalator.

Any other time Katie would have been delighted with the restaurant, which was large and elegant and filled with attractive people. Her mother spoiled it for her. She said nothing on the trip from Wanamaker's and wouldn't meet Katie's eyes as they were shown to their table in the restaurant. That meant she was going to get a lecture later, the same old lecture about being a proper southern gentlewoman and not a vain silly goose.

Never mind that. Jake liked her. She clung to the memory of that wonderful few minutes with desperation. When her mother finally spoke, tell-

ing her that everyone had ordered, she chose the
first thing she saw and sat back in her chair ignoring all of them. If she could only forget the
amused looks on all their faces, except her
mother's, back at the store. It was that sneaky
Paige's fault. She had led them there on purpose
to embarrass her, to make her feel like a fool.

The salads came and Katie picked at hers,
watching her brother put on his perfect gentleman
routine. She knew how much of *that* was just an
act!

He chased the last radish in his salad around
the bowl until he finally speared it on his fork.
He popped it into his mouth and grinned at Paige.
"For a minute there, I thought I was going to lose
that fight," he said in a tone of mock relief.

When Paige smiled, she bent her head forward. Her shining hair swayed over her cheek,
half hiding her face. For a split second a poster in
the art room back in Atlanta flashed in Katie's
mind. The artist had been Degas. For that moment, Paige, with her slender, curving neck and
dark eyelashes covering her eyes, could have been
the model for the ballerina in the picture.

Then the awful scene in the store flashed in
Katie's mind, and she felt her face redden. She
was being ridiculous even to *think* of Paige as
graceful. She was gawky and plain and went out
of her way to make other people uncomfortable.
She probably just posed like that, trying to make
people forget how long her neck was and the fact
that she didn't even show her teeth when she
smiled.

How could Tuck act so animated with only Paige to talk to? She was probably making him sick, too, and he was too much of a gentleman to let on. Maybe he hadn't had a chance to find out how dull she was, because he was doing all the talking himself. As Katie glared at him, he began to tell Paige another story about life in Atlanta.

Across the table Katie's mother was laughing softly at something Mr. Whitman had said. Megan and Mary Emily were having a race to see who could eat buttered hard rolls the fastest.

I hate this place, Katie told herself. The music was dull. The people at the other tables were all wrapped up in each other, and the food was slow in coming. If this were in Atlanta, at least one group of friends would come in and stop at their table to talk to them. Nobody even seemed to know she was alive in this place. She could probably just fall under the table without anyone noticing.

As she looked back, most of the day seemed long and dull and pointless. Not one really fun thing had happened since early morning. She caught her breath, remembering. Maybe meeting someone like Jake was all the excitement anyone could ask for in a single day. What a handsome boy — almost mysterious. She wanted to close her eyes and relive that wonderful time all over again; Jake looking up at her and stopping as if turned to stone for that long, silent moment.

Katie glanced up to see her mother looking at her. Katie forced a little smile, hoping it might help later. Only when Virginia Mae smiled back and turned away, did Katie realize what she had done. She had smiled in that tight closed-lips way, just as Paige had done. Horrors! She absolutely must *not* catch the miserable habit of simpering instead of smiling, the way Paige Whitman did!

CHAPTER 8

Katie could tell from Paige's even breathing across the room that her stepsister had fallen asleep at once. In spite of the busy day just behind her, Katie Summer couldn't get to sleep. Oh, what she wouldn't give to be back home in Atlanta with her friends. She had never realized how important it was to have close friends to talk to. How lonely it felt to have a wonderful, romantic thing happen to you and not have a single person to tell it to!

But it was impossible to tell anyone in her family. Mary Emily would promise faithfully to keep it a secret, then let it out with looks and gestures. Tuck would jump on her again for being fickle. Her mother would think of some reason to disapprove, just as she had disapproved of every single thing Katie had done or said or worn all day long.

But if she were back home in Atlanta, she could call her best friend Jill. Jill would want to hear every word about her meeting Jake Carson. She would be as excited as Katie herself about the way he had acted when he first saw her. Jill had always believed in love at first sight. Katie could imagine the way she would crow with delight and cry out, "I told you so! Didn't I tell you so?"

Jill had every right to laugh at her, too. She and Katie had talked about instant love for years, with Katie always claiming it was impossible. "A boy has to be more than good-looking for me to fall in love with him," she had protested. "He has to know how to treat a girl, be smart enough to be interesting company, have a good sense of humor, and be able to dance."

But Jake was not only smashing to look at, you could tell right away he was all those other things, plus a lot more. How mysteriously disturbed his face had looked at first, and how much she had wanted to get close enough to him to comfort him.

The way she felt was wild and wonderful and too overwhelming to keep to herself.

She stirred and turned her pillow over. Binker moved, too. She stroked the cat's soft fur and whispered, "Tomorrow. I will get to see Jake Carson again tomorrow."

When the sunlight pouring through the tall windows wakened her, Katie sat up instantly. The other bed was already empty. Katie felt a quick surge of hope. Maybe Paige was already out running her dog, and Katie wouldn't even have to see her before breakfast.

No such luck. The door to the bathroom they

shared was locked, and Katie heard the sound of rushing water from inside.

It wasn't the end of the world. She had to decide what to wear anyway. Her mother had hardly let her pack anything, because the rest of their things were coming along right away. By the time Paige unlocked the door and came out, Katie had decided on bright flowered shorts and a yellow high neck, sleeveless top and had her bed all made.

At breakfast, Mr. Whitman suggested they all spend the morning at the zoo in Fairmount Park. "Or if you would rather, we could drive around and look over both of your schools." He smiled at the younger girls who were grinning at each other. "Megan is burning up to have Mary Emily see her old stamping grounds."

For a wild moment Katie's heart sank. That wasn't the way she had pictured her day at all. Luckily she recovered quickly enough to speak up instantly. "If you don't mind, I'll pass. I have a lot of things to do here today, and we have all of next week to do that, don't we?"

She ignored the puzzled look on her mother's face and went on swiftly. "I need to get Binker settled in, fix my drawers, and I would just love to hang out and relax."

"I almost forgot about your cat," Mr. Whitman admitted. "Has she ever even ventured downstairs?"

Tuck shook his head. "It's better that she doesn't for a while," he said. "I'd hate to see Binker tangle with a dog as big as Scarlett."

"What an awful thing to say!" Mary Emily protested. "You know they're going to be good friends, just the way we all are."

The house seemed awfully quiet after the family left. Katie helped Miss Aggie clear the table and put away dishes, then went outside. After prowling around the yard and petting the dog without seeing any sign of Jake Carson, she came back inside. She wanted to ask Miss Aggie when Jake was coming, but she didn't want to seem that interested.

By eleven o'clock, she gave up on his coming at all. I can't believe I was stupid enough to get up early for nothing, she scolded herself. Could he possibly be staying away because she had been so quick to say she would like to see more of him, too?

The only way to shove Jake out of her mind was to keep busy. She cleaned Binker's litter box and found a good place for it in an alcove in the hall. She brushed the cat's long, silky fur until it rose straight up into the air after the brush and crackled with static electricity. It was so boring and dull in the quiet house that she would even be glad to see the family come back. By the time they finally *did* come, a little after twelve-thirty, Katie decided that if things didn't get a little livelier, she could be dead of boredom before school even started.

Katie carefully waited until lunch was almost over to say anything. "I didn't see Jake out there this morning," she told her stepfather.

"He doesn't come on Tuesdays or Thursdays,"

Megan explained. "We're not the only job he has."

Katie had seen Paige look up at her when she asked the question. When Katie glanced over at her, Paige dropped her gaze down at her plate. Katie stared at her thoughtfully. Was it possible that Paige had a crush on Jake? She decided against it. After all, they were just friends, Jake had said so himself. And he hadn't acted in any special way about Paige, just lumping her in with all the Whitmans.

The day lasted forever, and the day after was not a whole lot better. Jake did come on Wednesday, but she barely had a word with him before Mr. Whitman came out with Tuck, and the three of them went off to rearrange the double garage to make space to store the extra bikes and the trunks that were to arrive with the rest of the Guthrie things.

The moving van from Atlanta arrived on Thursday. To hear Mary Emily and Megan, you would have thought it was Christmas. They giggled and squealed as they unpacked Mary Emily's trunk and worked on their room. They sounded so childish that Katie carefully concealed her own excitement at having her own things again. The last few days before the wedding she and her mother had finished shopping for her school clothes. She was wild about most of her new things and couldn't wait to get them out and try them on again.

But Megan and Mary Emily didn't care who knew how much fun they were having. They ran up and down the stairs a million times for thumb tacks and picture hangers and tools to work with. When Tuck finished unpacking his own trunk, they dragged him in to help. "Don't anybody look!" Mary Emily warned when Katie came out into the hall. "We want it to be a surprise!"

Her own room was surprise enough for Katie. She had been right about the space; there wasn't any. When she had put all her folding things into her share of the drawers, she had a ton of important items left over, all her makeup, her monogrammed jewelry box and earring stand, and her ruffled basket of perfume samples.

If Paige had been around, Katie really might have checked with her about using the whole top of the dresser. But Paige never even stuck her head in, and she obviously didn't wear makeup. If she wore earrings, Katie hadn't seen them. She shrugged and set her own things out, even though that left no room for Paige's belongings.

As Katie worked, she kept hearing the phone ring down the hall. Each time it rang she stopped to listen from force of habit. At home she got most of the calls. But none of these calls were for her. Instead, Miss Aggie called for either Paige or Megan, and Katie went back drearily to unpacking her things. At home her friends would be calling to talk about school opening, deciding how to dress, telling what had happened on vacation.

There was room in her half of the closet for only about half of her shoes. When she tried to hang up her clothes, she saw that Paige's were sticking over onto her half of the space. Since she couldn't stand to see her exciting new things smashed before she even got to wear them, she tied a red scarf very tightly at the middle of the closet bar to mark the halfway point. Even then, her clothes were so tightly pushed together that every single garment would have to be pressed.

Katie was near tears as she finished the job. The room was awful. It was crowded and dull and there was nothing in it to remind her of who she really was. Then, at the very bottom of the last box, she found the long satin ribbon she had always kept on the wall of her room in Atlanta.

She studied the walls for a place to hang it up. Paige's posters had taken all the good space. Finally she knocked on Megan's door and got thumb tacks to hang the ribbon between Paige's bulletin board and her framed DIVA poster.

Katie was just finished, when the little girls shouted for everyone to come up and see their masterpiece.

In spite of herself Katie laughed when she saw their door. They had lettered and hung up a sign that read "Meg and M.E."

"Get it?" Mary Emily asked. "*Meg* for Megan and the *M.E.* for my name. Say it fast — Meg-AndM.E. The *M.E.* stands for Mary Emily."

Katie's mother laughed and touched her daughter's shoulder. "You kids are too much!"

Their room really did look darling. Mary Emily's horse pictures were scattered in among Megan's movie posters. Stuffed animals from two collections filled a wall bookcase, with the extra ones cuddled in together in the rocking chair in the corner. Two low chairs faced a low square table. "For games," Megan explained. "Maybe sometimes puzzles, but mostly we'll play games together here."

A tired feeling swept over Katie. How could they be so happy together when she was so miserable with Paige?

Naturally everyone went to look at their room too. Megan was entranced by Katie Summer's things. She stood on tiptoe and stared at the basket of perfume. "Wow!" she breathed. "What do you do with all these?"

Katie was suddenly self-conscious, with Paige staring at her coldly from the door. "Well," she shrugged. "Different perfumes go with different personalities. After I decide who I want to be that day, I pick a perfume that goes with it."

Megan was still staring, fascinated, at the little bottles when Mary Emily tugged her across the room. "This is Katie's memory ribbon," she explained. "See all those things? That was the corsage Eric sent when they went to their first dance. These are favors from parties. Look at that darling fan. That was a Hawaiian party."

"My sister, the social butterfly," Tuck kidded her, but Katie knew he meant it.

Paige still hadn't moved or said a word. Katie felt waves of anger from her dark figure in the doorway. She breathed deeply and forced herself to smile at her mother. Was it her fault that Paige didn't have any exciting romantic memories to treasure?

Maybe if she'd loosen up and quit looking like the witch in a fairy story, she could be a social butterfly, too, instead of a dull stick of a girl.

CHAPTER 9

Saturday Jake worked in the yard all morning and had soup and sandwiches with the family at lunch. His dark eyes shone when Katie told him about the rowers. "I must have been about six when my dad first let me hang onto his oar," he told her. "I'll take you out, Katie. You'll love the river."

Paige said nothing. Katie's mother tried to draw her into the conversation, but it didn't work. She excused herself without dessert and went upstairs with some silly excuse that nobody could believe. Jake stared after her with puzzled eyes. Katie felt a moment of panic. Paige and Jake had been friends for a long time. The last thing Katie wanted was for Jake to ask Paige what was wrong, and then have Paige turn him against her. She thought wildly of some way to distract him and came up with a question that sounded innocent enough.

"I forgot to ask you what happens here in the winter," she said, leaning toward him. "Do you have lots of ice and snow? When we get two snowflakes back home, the entire city skids to a halt."

Jake looked at her and then laughed, a warm surprising laugh that lit up his whole face. "You're kidding."

"Oh no, she's not," Tuck assured him solemnly. "Snow is a real crisis in the city of Atlanta. They bring out all the snow equipment . . . two brooms."

Katie watched the two boys with satisfaction. Neither of them showed any sign of interest in why Paige had gone upstairs to sulk.

During the last week before the start of school, a lot of things changed. Mr. Whitman began going back to his office at least for part of each day. Tuck got interested in the city and prowled around a lot with a map and guidebook. Megan and Mary Emily played all over the house, from the basement to the attic without a hint of a cross word between them. Even Katie's mother relaxed and began playing the piano again, apparently as happy and comfortable in her new home as she had been back in their own apartment in Atlanta.

Katie *didn't* feel comfortable. She couldn't relax. Her only good times were the days when Jake was there to work. He seemed to have a million jobs to do around the Whitman house and all of them different. One day while he was working in the back garden, she sat in the sun watching him break the lawn mower down into pieces and clean and oil the parts.

"I can't get over how many things you know how to do," she told him, genuinely impressed.

"I like knowing how things work."

"That's all very well if you *have* to do it," she said. "But machinery like that? Where did you learn to do that?"

He leaned on the handle of the mower and laughed at her. "From lying under cars, watching men work with machinery."

She studied him silently a minute. Mr. Whitman had said he came from an old Philadelphia family that had produced a lot of outstanding people. It still seemed funny that he chose to do hard physical work.

"And you'd rather do this than go to college?"

He wiped his hands on a filthy cloth. "I'm going to college, but it was silly to go before I was ready. I can't remember doing anything but going to school. I needed to take a year off and just see if I could make it, sort of find out who I was."

"You're Jake Carson," she whispered, smiling and leaning toward him as if she were revealing a great secret.

His hands stopped as he looked directly at her. His eyes changed somehow. For a moment it was as if a force, something like a charge of electricity passed between them. Katie felt her heart begin to beat so rapidly that she wondered if he could hear it. When she dropped her eyes, the spell broke and he spoke almost roughly, as if he were angry. "You're really something else, Katie Summer." He shook his head as if he were trying to rid himself of something.

She could tell he was trying to make his words sound light when he spoke again. "How come I never met anybody like you before?" he asked in a flippant tone.

She barely trusted her voice but answered him anyway, mimicking his tone. "How come I never met a guy like you?"

He looked up at her again, and that shivery sense of tension was back, just like that. Nothing he did or said would have surprised her. She caught her breath silently as his expression turned cold and unreadable, as if he were shutting her away.

"Don't do that," she cried.

"What?" his tone was casual and he looked back down at his work.

"Get that icy look on your face," she told him. "It scares me."

He rose and started across the lawn with the oil can. "It better scare both of us," he said harshly. "We have no business starting anything between us. We're too different, Katie. Look at you, you're only fifteen and I'm eighteen, out of school, the whole bit. We're flat dead wrong for each other, and we both know it."

She followed him across the lawn. "*I* don't know it!" she told him.

"I just told you." From his tone he could have disliked her. Quick, hot tears pressed behind her eyes. This wasn't fair.

She hesitated in the door of the garage. "Anyway," she told him. "*You* started it. Why did you come on to me that first morning if I was so wrong for you?"

He turned and stared at her. The light was so dim that she couldn't read his expression. "I shouldn't have," he said quietly. "I had no business doing that." For an incredible instant, she thought he was going to take her in his arms, and she wanted him to more than anything in the world.

Instead, he stepped farther away and turned his back to her, fiddling with something on the work bench. "I was wrong," he repeated angrily. Then, as if to keep her from saying anything back, his tone turned clipped and businesslike. "Do me a favor, will you, Katie? Ask Tuck if he'll give me a hand washing the cars?"

She hesitated a moment, trying to read his face. It was useless. She turned and went into the house to get Tuck. Why couldn't she understand him the way she had always understood boys? He gave such conflicting signals. One minute she thought she could read in his eyes that he really liked her, the next they might be enemies for the way he treated her. He had sent her off like a child on an errand, but even that didn't keep her from being more interested in him than she had ever been in a boy before. If she could just know how he *really* felt about her!

But she couldn't hang out with Jake all the time, and on the days he didn't come her loneliness for her old friends deepened steadily. More and more calls came for Paige. Her friends were coming home from summer camp or their family places at the beach and called to talk endlessly. Katie didn't mean to listen, but she kept hearing snatches of conversation and knew Paige's friends were asking how it was with her new stepmother, stepbrother, and stepsisters.

If she were in Atlanta her friends would be asking the same questions. She shuddered to think what Paige was going to say about her when she had private time with her friends. As it was, sometimes Paige fell silent when Katie walked into the room, and she was certain Paige had been talking about her.

Tuesday it rained, a slow, steady rain that darkened the house like a cave. Katie went upstairs to curl up with her music only to find that it didn't help. Love songs made her want Jake to come back and sad songs reminded her of her own misery. How could she be so shut out and lonely? She wasn't a bad person, she was just herself. Was there any crime in laughing and joking and living life every day as happily as you could?

She couldn't even stand to look around the room she shared with Paige. It was a mess, as usual, with Paige's bed unmade and her robe falling off onto the floor. Her mother always carried on about *her* being a southern lady . . . did a lady have to live in a human pig pen? She took off her headphones and threw herself across the bed. She might have cried if she hadn't glanced at the closet. Paige had left the door open, as usual. Katie stared at the closet in disbelief. Paige had shoved Katie's things clear over, bunching them all up in about a third of the space.

She sat up and wanted to scream. Instead she

stared thoughtfully at the closet bar for a moment. She could stop that! She dug behind her shoes in the back of the closet for her art box. She used a ruler and measured carefully, to the inch, then smeared super glue on the red scarf and pressed it onto the closet rod until she was sure it would set like a rock.

Mary Emily came flying through the door while she was still holding the scarf in place.

"What's the red flag for?" she asked.

"It's not a red flag," Katie snapped at her. "It's my scarf and it marks the boundary between Paige's space and mine. Something Paige can't figure out, obviously!"

"It *looks* like a red flag," Mary Emily said. Then she shrugged. "Mom wants to talk to you downstairs. She's in the living room."

As she flipped out the door, Katie felt a rush of excitement. This waiting was almost over. If she could only get through until school started, she just knew it would be easier. She had always been popular at school. Why should it be any different in Philadelphia?

Paige saw the red scarf tied in the center of the closet bar when she went upstairs for her denim jacket. She grasped the red cloth and jerked hard. To her astonishment, the sturdy fabric ripped along one side but still didn't budge from the wooden pole. All the ugly words Paige had ever heard one girl call another streamed silently through her mind.

Never mind *what* Katie Summer Guthrie was, she had won another round.

Not that Paige hadn't asked for this one. Seeing Katie with Jake had made Paige lose her control. What she wanted to do was tear all Katie's clothes to shreds and pile them on the floor. Instead, she had done the only thing she dared . . . slam all those bright new outfits back into Katie's space and hope they wrinkled so badly they would never iron out. Even tearing up the clothes wouldn't have helped. Nothing was going to help.

Paige tugged her jacket on, feeling a little ill. She would give anything in the world to be able to forget the way Jake and Katie had stood and talked. Talked! Neither of them were saying a word. They just stood very close, looking into each other's eyes.

She groaned and started downstairs to get Scarlett for a run in the park, leaving the red flag torn but still firmly glued in the center of the closet.

At the bottom of the stairs she paused. Through the closed door of the living room she heard voices, first Katie's then Virginia Mae's. They were arguing. Paige couldn't make out any words but the tones were plain enough. Virginia Mae's voice firm and disapproving, Katie's voice rising, tearful, and out of control. Paige walked swiftly through the hall. The last thing she wanted was to be caught eavesdropping.

The one big happy family business wasn't working. Everybody in the entire house except her father knew it wasn't working. Well, she corrected herself, maybe the little girls hadn't picked up the tension yet. That was probably a good thing. At least *someone* was getting something good out of this stupid, ridiculous marriage!

Scarlett barked hysterically in greeting. Paige wrestled the leash onto her, trying to twist her face away from the dog's eager kisses. By the time she was down the hill and into the park, her face was stinging from tears of helplessness. Tears weren't going to help. Jake didn't just *like* Katie, he had fallen for her. Paige knew it.

And I miss my dad, Paige told herself miserably as Scarlett snuffled at a bush imagining a rabbit. She never had any time alone with him anymore. But even if she did, what could she say?

"I love your wife and the other kids, but ship that Katie Summer off somewhere, or I'm going to die?"

From what Mary Emily had suggested, Katie naturally thought her mother wanted to talk about the beginning of school. The minute she entered the living room and saw her mother, she knew she'd guessed wrong. Whenever her mother had to do something really unpleasant, she stood very straight, as if she could stiffen her resolve along with her backbone. When Katie entered, her mother turned to her without smiling.

"Is something the matter?" Katie asked.

"Please close the door behind you," her mother said. "Then come over and sit down."

"I *know* something's wrong," Katie said, sitting down on the far end of the divan. "Is it something back home? Is Grandma sick?"

Her mother sat down across from her "Something is wrong, Katie, and it is here at your home. *This* is your home now, not Atlanta. And I am really upset about the way you're acting. You know that I would rather not call you down in front of your new family, but you are taking terrible advantage of my attempts to be kind to you."

Katie leaped to her feet without thinking. "What are you talking about? What have I done that's so awful?"

"Sit down, Katie," her mother said firmly. "And quit shouting at me. I'm willing to overlook how bad your manners have been since we came here, but I am not willing to see you treat Paige the way you do. You are barely civil to her. You've done nothing but complain about that room since we got here. After all, it was Paige's room and she made every effort to share it half and half. And that business of going off by yourself at the park, and then staying so long in the bathroom that Paige had to go out with wet hair. You do one thoughtless, selfish thing after another."

"Selfish!" Katie cried. "Think how *I* feel! I'm not used to sharing a bathroom."

"Katie, please lower your voice. You are not a child anymore. You have to start behaving like a young — "

"Don't say it," Katie wailed. "Don't start in on me with that business of being a real southern lady again. This really is the twentieth century. And this isn't the South. I refuse to be — "

"Katie Summer," her mother's tone scared Katie for a moment. "Please remember who you are talking to. I am giving you a fair warning that you have to meet this new situation with more grace and generosity than you have shown up to now."

Katie stared at her mother silently.

"If you don't," Virginia Mae went on, "we will all be very sorry."

"I'm sorry now," Katie said, suddenly fighting tears.

"I love you, and Tuck and Mary Emily love you," her mother said as if she hadn't heard Katie's words. "Give the rest of our family a chance to see the real, loving girl down inside."

"I said I was sorry *now*," Katie repeated.

"I heard you, but I refuse to believe that you'll give up this easily. We are a family now. Let's make it work."

"Then talk to Paige. Tell her I can't live in a pig pen. Tell her — "

Her mother rose. "Katie, don't force me to take away your privileges in order to make peace in this house."

Katie stared at her. Privileges. That meant going out with the family and maybe even Jake if he asked her. That could mean coming straight home from school after it started and never getting to fool around with friends.

"You're not being fair to me," Katie told her. "You're not being fair, and you're just picking on me for no reason at all. You don't even treat me like you used to. You never have anything to say to me anymore without a lecture tacked on."

Her mother stood stiff and silent, just looking at her. Katie felt her face getting hot with anger and resentment. Why wasn't her mother seeing what was happening? Paige was as much at fault as she was, but her mother was only taking it out on her. What had happened between them?

"I'm sorry you see it that way, Katie Summer," she said, her voice rising. "I want you to think seriously about what I have said. I *want* this family to *be* a family."

When Katie didn't reply, she sighed. "That's all, Katie."

Katie paused in the hall. Where could she go to hide her reddened eyes and her fury? If she went to her room, Paige was sure to come in and make a mess or just sit silently across from her.

Her clothes, that's what she would do, press some of those wrinkled clothes. The ironing board was always up in the laundry room in the basement. The room smelled wonderful, of soap and bleaches and those fragrant sheets of softener that Miss Aggie threw into the dryer when she dried the laundry.

CHAPTER 10

Katie had finished the third shirt and was lightly spraying starch on her full pink skirt when she heard steps on the stairs. She stiffened. If she had to deal with Paige right then, she wasn't responsible for what happened. Instead, Tuck appeared and leaned against the side of the door.

"When you get through, I have some shirts," he teased.

"A dollar apiece, just like the old days," she told him.

"My sister, the hold-up artist." He fell silent. She glanced at him. He looked suspiciously uncomfortable.

"If Mom sent you down here to lecture me some more, forget it. She's already made it plain where I stand with her."

"That's silly. You stand where you always did. She's just fighting very hard to make this thing work."

"It's working *fine* for her," Katie told him, slamming the iron down hard on the flap of the skirt pocket. "Why should she care who else is miserable?"

"Come on, Katie," he said firmly. "What about all those years Mom was lonely and unhappy? Did you care about that while you flipped around having fun? We owe her every bit of help we can give her now. And remember, Katie, this isn't some lightweight deal. Those people are married. We've got to help make it work."

She glared at him. "Big deal! You have to put up with it just one year. Then you get to go back down south to college, and be among friends, and forget the whole mess. For me it is a life sentence. Anyway, you have a stronger stomach for that Paige than I do. But then, you don't have to share space with her."

"What's the problem between you two, anyway?" he asked. Tuck wished he hadn't agreed to speak to Katie for his mother. This business between the girls didn't concern him, and he didn't want to be involved. He was too close to leaving home to be embroiled in these childish feuds.

Katie looked up at him angrily. "She hates me, for starters, and I return the favor."

He shook his head. "Katie, why do you have to be so emotional about everything?" he asked as he turned to leave.

"Emotional!" Katie exploded. "Half of the time, she doesn't even speak to me! And that room we have to share is a pig pen."

He sighed. "If you would just talk it out! You

78

and Paige *are* different, but she's bright and reasonable."

"And I'm stupid and unreasonable, I guess."

"Katie, come on! You are both great in different ways. I can't imagine changing Paige — "

"If you think *I* am going to change, you're crazy," she broke in.

"Katie Summer, I don't believe you. You've always been the original charmer who could melt icebergs when there was something you really wanted. Don't change, just make up to her a little . . . talk to her. This silent treatment is the pits."

His eyes on Katie's were demanding and his tone very cool, almost disgusted. That hurt. "Okay," she whispered finally. "I'll try. But don't make any bets on it working."

He leaned over to thump her shoulder gently. "Hey. Now that's my Katie Summer. This means too much to blow it. Now I have to split . . . things to do."

Katie finished ironing the last of her things and took them up to hang in the closet. With Binker curled beside her, she turned on her radio, and settled on her bed to do her nails. When her favorite group came on she turned up the volume to hear better. She didn't hear Paige come in. Before Katie even knew she was there, the music stopped. Paige had simply leaned over and snapped off the radio.

She spoke, her tone icy, "Dinner's ready."

"Paige," Katie said quickly. "I really want to talk to you."

Paige had already turned her back. "Dinner is ready," she repeated, walking out, as if she hadn't even heard Katie.

Miss Aggie was a wonderful cook. The roast was tender and delicious and was served with tiny potatoes and carrots in rich brown gravy. Katie ate quietly, listening to the conversation around the table. On the surface it all looked so civilized. Tuck told Mr. Whitman about watching the ships in the harbor. Paige told what she probably thought was a funny story of Scarlett's vain attempt to out-run a rabbit. They sounded like a family series on TV, all loving kindness and nurturing. She glanced up to see her mother smiling at Paige and Katie hurt inside.

She knew she wasn't the "perfect southern lady" her mother had always wanted her to be. In other words, Katie thought crossly, I'm not stuffy and old fashioned and so sweet that sugar wouldn't melt in my mouth. But neither was Paige all that perfect. Virginia Mae was being fooled. She had no idea how petty and mean Paige could be.

And Paige managed to call her mother "Mom" about every other breath. She said it as if she really had a right to. As if Virginia Mae could ever in this life have a dark, dowdy creature like Paige for a daughter. It made Katie sick to her stomach.

She looked up, startled to realize her mother had apparently called her name twice. "Tuck is going to take Megan and Mary Emily horseback riding tomorrow, Katie. We wondered if you would like to go along."

Katie stared at her. Tomorrow would be Thursday, and Jake wouldn't come to the house anyway. "I'd love to," she said. "What about everybody else?"

"Bill has to go to court," her mother said. "I have some things I need to do here. Paige hasn't decided."

"That sounds like fun," Katie said. She smiled at Tuck. See? She tried to tell him with her eyes. See me trying to get along better?

Paige stood beside her stepmother and watched the station wagon disappear down the street. Virginia Mae hugged Paige and laughed. "How wonderful! We're going to have our first real time alone together. You are sure you wouldn't rather go ride with the others?"

"Positive," Paige nodded. "It sounds like fun, but I really have stuff I need to do."

Virginia Mae smiled. "Me, too, but let's go sit a minute and get our energy up. Those two little kids are like a whirlwind."

Paige laughed and got herself a diet cola while Virginia Mae filled her coffee cup again.

"Those little girls could pass for twins dressed alike the way they are," Miss Aggie said. "Of course there's the difference in their hair color . . ."

"And their faces," Paige added.

"And their accents," Virginia Mae put in.

Miss Aggie laughed genially. "They're sure cute, and Megan tells me they are going to dress alike all their lives."

Virginia Mae groaned. Paige listened idly, as her stepmother and Miss Aggie kidded about the problem of matching outfits for a redhead like Megan and a blonde like Mary Emily. "Lucky thing that jeans comes in basic blue," Miss Aggie said, picking up her cleaning basket to start upstairs.

How comfortable it was to be here at home with Katie gone. How clever she had been to stay undecided until she heard what her stepsister meant to do. How wonderful to have the whole day stretching peacefully ahead of her.

The day was fun. Miss Aggie had made up a market list, and Paige offered to go along to the store with Virginia Mae.

"Are you sure you want to?" she asked.

"I like grocery shopping," Paige admitted. "It always confused Dad, so Miss Aggie and I worked it out together."

Virginia Mae's eyes were tender on her. "You've been such a wonderful daughter to him, Paige. If I didn't love you for any other reason, I would because of what you mean to Bill."

Paige felt a thickness in her throat. What could she say? No wonder her father loved this beautiful woman. Probably her own mother would have loved her, too, if she had known her.

The day passed all too quickly. Late in the afternoon, Paige realized that she hadn't touched the piano keys since the wedding. When she sat down and played the first chords, Miss Aggie came to the door and smiled.

"Now *that's* my girl," she said quietly.

Paige had played through all her recital pieces and was just fooling around with her favorite songs when Virginia Mae came into the room.

"Don't stop," she said quickly. "I love hearing you play. You have such a sensitive touch. And we seem to like the same things."

"Which ones?" Paige asked.

"The Cole Porter tunes," Virginia Mae said, coming over to stand beside her.

"They're Dad's favorites," Paige laughed. "Do you know this one?"

As her fingers sped over the keys, Virginia Mae came around and sat on the bench beside her. "Do I? Let's try a duet."

Paige couldn't remember ever having more fun playing with anyone. They patched up a medley that lasted almost a half hour. They were pounding so loudly that they didn't hear the rest of the family come in. When Tuck began to applaud, they both exploded into laughter.

"What a team!" Tuck said, still clapping. "You're wonderful!"

"Private concerts only," Virginia Mae said, rising. "How was your day?" She paused. "And where are the girls?"

Tuck turned and looked around. "I thought Katie was right behind me, but I guess not. The little guys raced upstairs to settle who got the first shower."

Paige rose and put away the music. Katie Summer *had* been right behind him as he came through the hall. Paige had seen her stare at Paige at the piano with her mother and turn away with a look of pure fury on her face.

Katie fled up the stairs, flaming with jealousy. What a pretty scene that was! If Paige had set out to make Katie look as bad as possible, she couldn't have picked a better way.

Being a musician herself, her mother had wanted all of them to be the same, but it took too much time, and Katie knew she had no talent. Her mother should be happy now. She had Paige, and she could have her, as far as Katie was concerned.

She was almost to the top of the stairs when she heard her stepfather come in through the back. At the same moment, Miss Aggie came to the kitchen door and called up to her.

"Just a minute, Katie. You had a call while you were out." Before Katie recovered from her astonishment, Miss Aggie went on. "It was Jake Carson. He said he'd come by about five." She glanced at the clock. "Should be here any minute now!"

Katie was amazed. Jake coming to see *her*?

Katie caught her breath. "Oh, look at me! I'm a perfect mess. I've got to clean up." Her breath came short all of a sudden. She couldn't stand to have Jake see her like this.

Katie's hands trembled so much with excitement that she barely got fresh lip gloss on and pulled a brush through her golden hair before she heard Tuck call. "Katie, Jake's here to see you."

Only the little girls were missing from the downstairs. How embarrassing it was for a boy to have to face all those people when he came to see you!

But even though Mr. Whitman was talking to him, Jake watched her walk all the way down the stairs.

"Hi, Jake," she said with surprise.

"Hi, yourself," he said, unsmiling.

Mr. Whitman looked at both of them, then took his wife's hand. "I guess we should clear out and let you kids talk."

"Oh, no," Jake said quickly, his color changing just a little. "I wanted Katie to take in a movie with me tonight, if it's okay with you."

Katie looked at him in astonishment. *This*, after that cross speech about them being wrong for each other. His eyes were unreadable as he returned her glance. Her mother's reaction was plain enough. She frowned in a way that made Katie's heart plunge. "It's nothing personal, Jake," Virginia Mae said slowly. "It's just, well, we're so new here."

Mr. Whitman touched his wife's arm. "Katie couldn't break the ice in a new town in better company than with Jake," he said. "Ask Paige. She and Jake have been friends for over a year."

Virginia Mae bit her lip. "Even a double date would be different somehow." She turned to look at Paige who still sat on the piano bench, her face expressionless. "That would be fine! Paige, I know you've got some special friend who would love to have you call."

Katie groaned inwardly. Double dating with Paige? The thought was horrifying. For a moment she thought she was saved. Paige flushed a deep red, a clear admission that she didn't have a single boyfriend in the world she dared to call up.

Jake's eyes were still on hers, patient but a little amused. Maybe after all? But Katie should have known her mother wasn't through. Virginia Mae turned to Tuck, her voice bright and coaxing. "No problem. Tuck would be delighted to go with Paige, wouldn't you, Tuck?"

Katie barely breathed, hoping that just once Tuck would be flat-out honest with his mother and tell her he didn't want to. Katie could see Tuck was tempted by the way his neck stiffened and his face reddened just a little. He might even have made some excuse except that Paige's father got into the act.

"Great idea, Virginia Mae," he said jovially. Then he laughed. "Listen to us, running Katie's life for her. For all we know she doesn't even want to go!"

He herded the rest of the family out, leaving Jake and Katie alone. Jake stared down at her. "Better a cast of thousands than nothing, I guess. What do you say?"

"Why did you call? I thought you felt we were wrong for each other," Katie said.

"I do," Jake answered quickly. "But . . . well I'm here, aren't I?"

"Yes, you're here. In spite of yourself?" Katie asked.

"In spite of myself," Jake agreed. "Pick you up at seven?"

"Perfect," she answered.

After she let him out, she stood against the door for a long moment, just enjoying the shock waves of wonder he left her with.

CHAPTER 11

Paige felt a physical shock when she heard Miss Aggie give Katie Jake's message. Her hands were suddenly cold. She was so cold all over that she had to tighten her muscles to keep from shivering.

She should have been prepared, but she wasn't. She had guessed that Jake would be bowled over by Katie. Still, to have this public proof that her worst fears were confirmed was almost more than she could handle.

Dinner was strange. Katie bolted her food, then ran to get dressed. Her mother excused herself after a few minutes and went upstairs, too. Apparently they had a talk because when Virginia Mae came back down, Paige heard Katie banging the drawers and the closet door as if she were getting dressed all over again.

Paige tried to keep herself from looking at what Katie finally wore, but her eyes wouldn't stay away. The skirt was a clear vibrant blue, the color

of her eyes. The top was a soft cotton sweater
with a V neckline. Katie wore a single pearl on
a gold chain that glowed against her golden skin.
Her earrings matched the necklace, and she was
carrying a white scarf with soft fringe. Her panty
hose were even pale blue.

Katie had apparently decided to be somebody
glamorous that night, because when she came
down the stairs the hall was filled with a rich, ex-
pensive, heavy perfume from one of the bottles in
the ruffled basket.

Paige knew her dark blue pleated skirt wasn't
too dowdy and the white blazer went well with it.
She wished she had pumps with higher heels, but
Tuck was the first boy she had ever been out with
who was tall enough for her to wear anything but
nearly flats. She felt anonymous.

She would have felt one hundred percent worse
except for Tuck's gallantry. Even though Paige
was sure he didn't want to be there, he played the
most charming date in the city. His manners made
Prince Charles look like a country bumpkin. His
light banter kept her from dissolving into tears
as Katie clung to Jake's arm, smiled, leaned
against him, and generally couldn't keep her eyes
off him.

Fortunately for Paige, parts of the movie were
very sad. Since she wasn't the only person in the
audience fighting tears, she was less embarrassed
than she might have been by her reddened eyes
when they stopped for pizza later. Paige felt Tuck
getting increasingly more restless as they sat
watching Jake and Katie dance to music from
the juke box.

When he deliberately shifted his chair to look the other way, she stared at him, astonished.

"Don't get me wrong. I work at being loyal to my sister but sometimes it's hard labor. So far she hasn't figured out what problems fun and games can lead to. But she's young. I'll hold high hopes."

Paige was speechless. His expression didn't look very hopeful. He sounded critical and detached. There was more to Tuck than met the eye.

Until Friday morning, Paige hadn't realized how trapped she felt in the house she had always loved. When the phone rang during breakfast, Miss Aggie covered it with her hand and turned to Paige. "It's Judy Belnap. Shall I ask her to call back?"

"Judy!" Paige's dad said, looking up and smiling. "Where has that kid been all summer?"

"With her family at Cape Cod," Paige told him, half rising. "I'll take it in the other room."

"Give her my best," her father said heartily.

"Wow!" Judy said. "For a minute I thought I wasn't going to get to you in time. Now listen fast. Can you get away, with the new family and all?"

"I think I can. What's up?"

"You remember my cousin Andy from upper New York State?"

Paige giggled. "The tall one with all the teeth and the red hair?"

Judy laughed. "Time has worked its wonders. He starts in the Naval Academy at Annapolis next week and is here until Sunday. When Dad suggested going for a sail, Andy asked if you could be invited to come along."

When Paige hesitated, Judy's tone turned coaxing. "I'm dying to see you, and you *know* you want to get away. We'll have lunch on the boat and probably have you back home by three. Tell your dad I will pout forever if he doesn't let you come."

"Can I call you back?"

"Not possible," Judy's voice was breathless. "If you can make it, we'll be by for you right away. You know dad!"

Paige smiled. "Hold a minute. I'll be right back."

Her father turned when she came to the door. "Something up?"

"Judy's invited me for the morning and lunch. What shall I tell her?"

Virginia Mae looked astonished. "For goodness sakes, Paige, go if you want. You must be dying to see your friend if she's been gone all summer."

"The words right out of my mouth." Paige's dad nodded. "Run tell her you'll go."

Judy whooped in Paige's ear at the news. "Great!" she said. "Andy will be pleased, and me, too. Given traffic, we'll probably be out in front of your house in twelve to fifteen minutes."

"I guess Bob Belnap is in a hurry," Bill Whitman said when she went back to the table. "He always is. Do you need to go get ready?"

Paige nodded, glancing down at her sandals. "I have to put on topsiders and get a jacket."

Jake had just come to work when the Belnap station wagon pulled up. He walked over to their

90

car, leaned against the window, and spoke to them. "Have fun," he told Paige as he held the door for her to get in.

For once Paige was glad that Judy was so effusive. She made room on the seat for Paige, hugged her as she sat down, and then leaned back for Andy to get a chance to say "Hello." All that business as the wagon pulled away kept Paige from looking back at the porch where she was sure that Katie Summer was standing, waiting for Jake.

The day was beautiful. "The kind of a day that would make a sailor of anyone," Mr. Belnap told her. It was sunny with just enough wind to keep the yawl clipping along with billowing sails.

And time had indeed worked wonders with cousin Andy. He was even taller than Tuck, and he had grown up to his teeth. His red hair, which she had remembered as a huge curly bush, didn't look half bad in a regulation Navy cut. More than that, she had forgotten how funny and appealing he was as a person. If she could only keep from comparing him to Jake, whose dark good looks made even someone as handsome as Andy seem pale and uninteresting!

But the day did one wonderful thing: Katie Summer faded to a dull discomfort instead of a steady pain. After lunch, Mr. Belnap insisted on cleaning the galley by himself. With Mrs. Belnap and Andy working the sails, Paige and Judy curled in the prow, alone together for the first time all day.

Paige had known the question was coming and had no idea what she could possibly say to her best friend. She knew she *should* be loyal to her family and cover up what was going on. But who could she talk to if not to Judy?

"Okay, Paige," Judy said, sitting cross-legged with her black curls tousled around her face. "How does it feel to have a stepmother?"

Paige blew her breath out slowly. That one was easy. "She's fabulous, pretty, talented, and simply wonderful to me. It even feels good to call her Mom."

Judy frowned thoughtfully. "If you're being honest, she must be a winner."

"She is a winner," Paige nodded. "You'll love her. I know you will."

"Then what about the kids?"

Paige hesitated. She might as well take the easy ones first. "Tuck is a senior and a really nice guy. He's so thoughtful that I'm spoiled for life already. We get along fine. Mary Emily is a doll. She's Megan's age and they love each other."

"That's only two kids," Judy reminded her.

Paige hesitated again. "Katie Summer is the other one . . . blonde, blue eyes. Imagine my exact opposite at fifteen, and smashingly beautiful, and you've got Katie Summer."

"But what is she like?"

"Listen, Judy," Paige began. "Everything I say about Katie Summer has to be in absolute confidence. Promise! The marriage is done, that girl has moved in with me. Somehow I have to learn to live with Katie Summer Guthrie if it kills me."

When Judy moved closer and put her arm

around Paige, Paige groaned. "Now look, I'm going to cry, and I don't want to. But, Judy, I just can't believe that girl. She's horrible. Since they moved her into my room with me, I don't have any way to avoid her." The tears came sudden and swift. "I've never been so miserable in my whole life."

Judy fished a tissue from her pocket and hugged Paige. "Maybe it's just that way now. After all, you're older. Maybe she's trying to show off and will get better when she's been here a while."

Paige blew her nose and shook her head. "Believe me, she isn't impressed by me or anyone. She's really what she is. There's no way she's going to change the way she works. She comes off like a complete air head, but she's *not* as dumb as she makes out. She's smart enough to get her way about everything and wrap everybody in the world around her carefully manicured little finger. What she can't get done with smiles and batting her eyes, she manages with that silky little southern accent that's about two and a half steps away from baby talk. She makes me want to vomit every time she opens her mouth."

"But doesn't her mother talk the same way?"

Paige stared at her. "She may, but I don't notice it on her. And it's mutual. Katie despises me, too, and makes no secret of it."

"Your dad's no fool; he'll see what's going on and help you."

Paige shook her head. "My dad is blindly in love. He wants this marriage to work so badly that he can't see anything but that."

"I can't stand for you to be so unhappy," Judy said, staring out over the water. "I wish there was something I could do to help."

Paige tried to smile. "You can't imagine how much it helps just to get that all out to somebody. I was about to explode."

Mr. Belnap called up to them. "Two more hands needed here on deck." Judy leaped to her feet, brushed off her jeans, and tugged Paige to her feet.

"At least it sounds as if it can't get any worse," she said.

"I hope you're right," Paige told her.

A truck from Wanamaker's pulled in behind the Belnap station wagon as the Belnaps brought Paige home. "Can you come in and meet my new family?" Paige asked Judy's parents.

"There'll be time later," Mrs. Belnap said. "We loved seeing you, Paige. Come see us now that we're back home."

"And come to Annapolis, too," Andy urged her, taking her hand again and holding it longer than he needed to. She smiled at him, wishing the touch of his hand was half as exciting as just seeing Jake from a distance.

Jake Carson's car was still in the driveway and Paige wished she could avoid him. It was better not to see him at all than to see him with Katie hanging all over him like wet wash.

"You're back!" her father called from the living room.

"Me and a truck from Wanamaker's," she told him.

"Good. They called from the store an hour ago. Tuck and Jake have offered to hang the mirrors for me. They're out in back with Scarlett waiting for the delivery. Have a good time?"

"Fabulous!" Paige told him, starting upstairs. When she went in to get fresh jeans and a shirt, she found Katie racing madly around the room picking things up.

"The mirrors are here," Katie said, her arms full of books and clothing. "Aren't you going to help?"

"Dad said Jake and Tuck are putting them up," Paige told her. "I'm going to shower."

Katie got a strange look on her face and stopped dead still, staring at her. Paige frowned, then shrugged and went into the bathroom. Sailing was great but it always left her feeling gritty. As she started the shower she heard the boys' voices in the hall on the way to the little girls' room. Because they were there she hummed instead of singing, as she rinsed the salt from her hair and showered.

Katie watched Paige disappear into the bathroom in disbelief. Where was that girl's head? It wasn't normal not to have any pride, or shame . . . when you got right down to it. Personally, she would just die rather than let *anybody*, much less Jake, see her room looking the way theirs did.

She stared around at the room. The mess was all Paige's. Her bed was still unmade, of course. She had dropped her pajamas with a wet towel from her early shower. Her topsiders, damp with sea spray, were where she had slipped them off, with jeans and a shirt wadded beside them. Three pairs of shoes were on the floor next to some books and magazines.

"Very well, Miss Wonderful," Katie whispered to herself. She picked up all Paige's things, armfuls of them, and dumped them into an untidy tower on Paige's bed. From down the hall came Tuck's and Jake's voices and the tap of a hammer as they installed Megan's and Mary Emily's mirror.

Katie's day had already been frustrating enough. After her date with Jake the night before, she had really expected to have some time with him today. But he and Tuck had gone from one job to another, working together like old friends, leaving her out in the cold and acting as if they were the grown-ups and she was just another kid. Jake stayed for lunch, of course, but what kind of togetherness could you have with an entire family around the table.

And Paige. She hadn't thought much about it when Paige went flying off with her friend. Only gradually had she figured out from things Megan said that Paige was spending the day on a sailboat out on the ocean . . . a yawl, Megan called it.

Katie had never in her life been out on a sailboat in the ocean. It didn't seem fair.

"I have your mirror," Tuck called from the hall.

"Come on in," Katie answered.

Just as Tuck and Jake carried the heavy mirror in from the hall, Paige came out of the bathroom. Katie hid her smile. Her own side of the room was immaculate, the pillows plumped up, her books in a careful pile, even her casettes all back in their cases.

Tuck and Jake paused in the door and looked at the mess on Paige's bed. As they stood there, a tennis shoe Katie had thrown up there last slid off and fell to the floor with a thump.

"I don't believe this room," Tuck said. "Did a hurricane hit in here?"

Katie just shrugged, smiled at Jake, and said sweetly, "Everybody has his own style. Paige's happens to be total chaos."

Jake turned to Paige, still in the hall. "The things you can learn about an old friend," he teased her. "I would never have guessed you were Miss Piggy."

Paige flushed a deep painful red and couldn't meet his eyes.

Let her feel like a worm, Katie told herself triumphantly. It was her own doing. Her very own doing.

Before Paige could say anything, the hall was filled with the sound of frantic barking as Scarlett raced up the stairs in pursuit of the cat.

Mary Emily let out a shrill, terrified scream.

"Binker!" she cried. "Oh help, Tuck, help!"

CHAPTER 12

Scarlett was all over the upstairs hall, lunging and barking as the cat fled howling along the passage. Paige dived for the dog and tackled her. They went down together with Scarlett struggling and yelping to be freed.

Mr. Whitman was already halfway up the stairs with Virginia Mae right behind him. "What's happening?" he called. "Where did the dog come from? How did she get in?"

"I forgot to tie her up when the truck came," Tuck shouted over Scarlett's barking.

"And Tuck and I must not have closed the front door all the way," Jake added.

Mr. Whitman caught Scarlett's collar, pulled her away, and helped Paige to her feet. Both Megan and Mary Emily were wailing helplessly as Paige started down the stairs with the setter. Scarlett kept pulling back so hard that Paige had to drag her down a step at a time.

"Binker's gone," Mary Emily cried. "She's totally disappeared. We'll never see her again."

"That's ridiculous, Mary Emily," her mother told her. "The cat is here. She had nowhere else to go."

"Your mother's right," Mr. Whitman agreed. "Let Paige fasten up the dog while Jake and Tuck finish putting up the mirror. Then we'll all look for the cat. She has to be in the house somewhere."

"We might try the floor of Paige's half of the closet," Katie suggested softly. "Cats like dirty, dark places."

Katie hoped Jake saw the filthy look Paige shot up at her from the bottom of the stairs.

Even after everyone joined in the search, a half hour passed with no sign of the cat. "It's time for Jake to take off," Mr. Whitman said. "Binker has to be up here somewhere. Let's cool it a while. The poor thing is probably so scared she wouldn't come out now if her life depended on it. But the sooner things quiet down, the sooner she'll come out from wherever she's hiding."

"He's right, you know," Katie Summer agreed, following Jake and her parents downstairs.

Katie walked with Jake out to the driveway. He stopped beside his car and looked at her curiously. "What's up?"

She flushed. "I just wanted to tell you what a good time I had last night," she told him.

"I did, too," he said in a cool, formal tone. "Thanks for coming."

She hesitated. That was that? She felt curiously awkward having walked out with him for no more response than that. "I would have told you sooner, but we don't get much time alone."

"That's probably not all bad," he said.

Katie sighed inwardly. Why did he have to be like that, always giving her conflicting signals? "I could take offense at that remark, I guess," she told him, trying to conceal the hurt.

He opened the car door without comment. Just as she thought he was going to leave, he turned suddenly and took both her hands in his. His expression was solemn and his eyes cold. "You'd have to be pretty dumb not to know what I mean," he told her. "I've said it before, Katie. We have too many differences. Not only age, either."

She studied his face, feeling that rising excitement that always came at his touch. She *couldn't* be wrong. He was feeling just as she was. "So what *other* big difference have you come up with?" She asked, carefully keeping her tone teasing.

"Where we are in life. I have four years of college and three years of law school. I can't get involved with anyone. Especially someone like you, Katie. You want fun, and you should have it. I have to be serious to get where I want to be. I won't have time for playing. Find someone else, Katie."

She smiled up at him. "You *are* serious, aren't you?" she teased.

He dropped her hands and looked directly at her. "Katie, my grandfather is a lawyer, and my father is a lawyer. And they both are good ones, and I'm going to be just as good, maybe better.

100

My friends say I'm too ambitious, but that's who I am. How do you feel about that?"

Katie looked away, not knowing how she felt. "I don't know how I feel about *that*. I only know how I feel about *you*."

"They're one and the same," he said. But then when he saw the tears in her eyes, he caught her in his arms and held her very tight. She felt his heart beating hard against her own.

When his arms loosened, he bent his mouth to hers, kissing her in a hard, demanding way. Then, his mouth softened against hers in a tender, lingering caress. She clung to him, breathless, and lifted her hands to touch his hair, loving the springy, warm feel of it under her fingers. He was whispering her name over and over, "Katie. Katie."

This had to be what love was, being close to someone and never wanting to let go, she thought.

He released her and stepped back against the car. "This is crazy," he said in that harsh tone he had used before. "It doesn't make any sense."

"So maybe we're crazy about each other," she said brightly, knowing her voice sounded strange because of the way her heart was still pounding.

He shook his head. "No way, Katie. We're just acting irresponsibly. Hey, you're a high school kid. You're going to meet a hundred guys your own age as soon as that place opens up over there. What a time you're going to have!"

"I don't want any other guy," she cried. "You're talking nonsense."

"That makes two of us then," he said, getting into the car.

"Then there's a place we're *not* different," she taunted him. He groaned and started the motor. But he was smiling.

"Bye, Jake!" she called lightly, waving as he backed from the drive. The minute the car was out of sight, the life seemed to flow from her body. *He* might not be in love with her, but she knew how *she* felt. How could he kiss her in that desperate way if he didn't love her?

Upstairs, Paige looked at Mary Emily and Megan, who were tearstained and smeared from crying. "I don't mind looking a little longer."

"Okay! okay!" Tuck said impatiently, "I'll give it another ten minutes. But quit bawling, you two!"

With the girls tagging behind them, Tuck and Paige searched every inch of the entire second floor for what seemed the hundredth time.

Back in the hall again, Tuck leaned against the wall and slid down to sit on the floor, frowning. "This makes no sense at all," he told Paige. "Binker wouldn't have run downstairs with Scarlett coming up. She has to be up here somewhere. Is there some place we haven't looked?"

Paige started to shake her head, then wailed. "What's the matter with me? Why didn't I think? Tuck, there's a whole other floor above this one. We haven't even started in the attic."

The attic door at the back of the linen closet stood slightly ajar. Tuck was up the stairs in a minute with Paige and the little girls right behind him.

Mary Emily saw Binker first. The cat was

sitting calmly on a narrow attic window ledge, looking down at the pigeons on the roof. Mary Emily scooped the startled cat into her arms and hugged her tight. Then she glanced out the window and burst into giggles. Megan, beside her, petting the cat, peered out and did the same.

"What's so funny?" Tuck asked, stepping over behind them. Paige had never seen anyone's expression change so swiftly and so drastically. One minute he looked relieved and the next he looked startled. He turned swiftly, catching Paige's arm. "Let's go back down," he said.

He didn't catch Paige fast enough. The view through the window looked right into the driveway where Jake's car was parked. Katie and Jake were standing so close to each other that they seemed like one person. With their arms wound around each other, Katie raised her lips to his. Paige felt as if she were paralyzed. In that shattering moment she saw Katie's hand rise to stroke Jake's dark hair with a loving, possessive air. The sudden rush of pain made Paige so dizzy that she stumbled as she backed away.

Tuck caught her arm to steady her. "I'm sorry," he said with embarrassment. "I'm really awfully sorry."

Paige looked at him, suddenly terrified. He knew how she felt about Jake? Had she been that obvious?

"She always goes after what she wants, that Katie," Tuck said slowly.

CHAPTER 13

Tuck's words were puzzling to Paige that afternoon. She understood them all too well when school started the following Monday morning.

"We have all the enrollment paperwork done," her father said at breakfast. "Now it's up to you, Megan and Paige, to show our new family around your schools."

Megan and Mary Emily were both so excited about going to school together that they began to talk at the same time, full of plans they had hatched.

Paige was glad they took center stage. She needed that minute to disguise the horror she felt at the thought of dragging Katie Summer around her high school. And it wasn't entirely personal either. She would have wanted to stay as far as possible from *anyone* dressed the way Katie was. She was going to stand out like a beacon. Maybe they wore dressy clothes to school in Atlanta, but they sure didn't in Paige's high school. All those pastel colors! Just because Katie had the right to mess up her own life didn't give her the right to do the same to other people.

Tuck felt his own reluctance because he spoke up quickly. "Thanks, sir, but I don't need any help. I've been through the enrollment drill before, and none of us is even in the same class."

Mr. Whitman frowned. "I just thought it might help you both to have a private guide. That's a very big school." He grinned. "I'm sure even Paige got lost a few times when she first started going there."

"I can't *imagine* getting lost and not being able to meet somebody who'd be happy to help find me!" Katie said brightly.

Sick, Paige told herself. I am going to be sick.

Tuck had to smile. Leave it to Katie.

Katie was so glad to be starting school that she didn't even object when Tuck had her sit in the back seat with Megan and Mary Emily while he drove the little girls to their school. She hummed to herself as Megan and Mary Emily tumbled out of the car, unable to believe that this day had finally arrived.

Tuck looked worried, and Paige didn't look all that happy, but then she never did. Katie herself was so excited she could hardly sit still in the seat. A new school was like a whole new world. Maybe when she had new friends of her own, Paige wouldn't get on her nerves so badly. She could just ignore her and have a wonderful time, the way she had in Atlanta.

105

The high school parking lot was so crowded that Tuck had to circle several times before finding an open space. Katie stared around her, impressed in spite of herself. "This place is huge," she whispered out loud.

"Lots of kids drive the first few days," Paige said. "Just until their schedules settle down."

Katie stared at the back of Paige's head. If Paige thought Katie was going to ride the bus all the time, she was dead wrong. She was going to try out for the swim team first thing. Riding the bus was impossible with after-school practices. For one scary moment she wondered how good their swim team was and if she could make it this first year.

"You ready back there?" Tuck asked, looking at Katie as he killed the motor.

"One hundred percent," Katie told him.

Take that back. Make it about ninety percent. It would be a hundred percent if she could go in there alone or even just with Tuck. Trailing along with Paige certainly wasn't her idea of the way to make a smashing first impression.

Katie found that the problem of being saddled with Paige solved itself automatically. A huge sign announced that returning students were to meet in their first period classes. New students were to assemble in the auditorium in different areas according to grade level.

Katie found the sophomore group and looked around the noisy room with rising excitement. It *was* a big school, with what seemed like thousands of kids. Maybe she shouldn't judge all the girls in school by what the new enrollees were wearing, but the ones waiting in line were all borderline dowdy, wearing dull, conservative clothes she wouldn't be caught dead in. She looked down at the pink skirt and blouse she was wearing and felt a moment of panic. Maybe she was the one dressed peculiarly.

The enrollment was well organized. Within minutes, the students were separated into two groups. She was directed to a line on the left which included all the sophomores who had enrolled in advance. In no time at all she sat across the table from a pleasant-looking woman in a gray linen dress, whose name tag announced that she was Mrs. Foster, Assistant Principal.

"Welcome to our school," Mrs. Foster said. Then she read the information on the card. "Katie Summer Guthrie," She looked up with fresh interest. "You must be Paige Whitman's new sister."

"Yes, ma'am," Katie said, startled.

Mrs. Foster smiled broadly. "Welcome! Such a nice family, the Whitmans, and we have loved having Paige."

She pulled out Katie's card and reached for a folder.

"You must realize that students progress at different rates in different schools. We usually assign new students to a less demanding level to avoid the possible embarrassment of having to set them back. In your case, however, we've decided to start you in the top level. Of course you will be on probation until the end of the first

107

grading period, but we have confidence in your ability. We all know what an excellent student Paige is."

Katie listened to Mrs. Foster's speech with growing horror. But I'm not Paige, she wanted to cry out. I'm me.

Mrs. Foster went on. "I see you were on the swim team back in Atlanta. Since you are being placed in the top level, you are also qualified to try out for our team if you want to."

"Oh, I want to!" Katie said quickly. Then the woman's words really sank in. "Are you saying that if I don't stay in the top level I can't swim with the team?"

"That's right," Mrs. Foster said cheerfully. "Taking part in such activities is reserved for students who don't need extra study time. Now," she paused. "What are you called? You don't use your *whole* name, do you?"

"Yes, ma'am, I do," Katie replied.

Mrs. Foster tilted her head. "Now I want you to do what you really want to do, but it's possible you might drop back to just a single name here." She smiled warmly. "You're going to get kidded enough about that cute accent of yours, and double names are unusual in this area. Want me to put you down just as Katie?"

Katie hesitated. She liked her whole name. She thought it sounded right for her, sunny and bright. She hesitated. She could always change it back if she couldn't stand it. "I s'pose so, ma'am," she said reluctantly.

Mrs. Foster handed Katie's folder to a tall brunette girl at her side. "Katie, this is Jayne

Singleton, a classmate of Paige's. Jayne will see you to your first class."

Katie almost protested. She didn't want to be herded around like a kindergartner. And the girl was so stern and unsmiling that Katie didn't even want to walk down the hall with her. She caught herself in time and smiled. "Hello, Jayne," she said in the warmest tone she could muster.

She didn't even get a real answer. Jayne just grunted something and turned away, signaling Katie to follow. Right away Katie decided Jayne was a genuine grouch. She marched through the halls so fast that Katie had to skip once in a while to keep up with her. Katie felt awkward and angry by the time they got to the second floor. She had enough rudeness to deal with at home without this!

"What's the big rush?" Katie finally asked.

Jayne looked at her. "To get this over with."

"How come you're doing this if you don't like it?"

Jayne stared at her, grinned, and slowed down. "Good point. What a crazy accent! Where did you get it from anyway?"

"Atlanta, Georgia," Katie told her.

Jayne stopped and stared at her. "I must have heard wrong. I thought Mrs. Foster said you were Paige Whitman's *sister*."

"Stepsister," Katie corrected her. "My mother married her father last month."

Jayne stared a minute more, then nodded, and laughed. When she laughed her eyes shone, and she was almost pretty. "That explains it," she said.

At Katie's puzzled look, Jayne shrugged. "I

was having trouble dealing with how different you are from Paige Whitman."

Katie glared at her. One more mention of wonderful Paige Whitman and she was going to explode. "So I'm different!" she said, not caring that it sounded hostile.

Jayne looked over at her with surprise. "Don't be huffy. I meant that as a compliment. This is Miss Palmroy's room. You should be able to follow your schedule from here."

Katie stood staring after Jayne a moment. It was wonderful to know that one person in the world beside herself didn't think Paige Whitman was so great.

Paige and Judy Belnap managed to get chairs next to each other in their first period English class and compare the print-outs of their schedules. "We only have two classes together," Judy complained. "We've *got* to get adjoining lockers."

"We will," Paige assured her. "We get to keep our old numbers."

Paige looked up to see Judy studying her thoughtfully. "I saw you come in with your new family," Judy said. "Your stepbrother is a real fox."

Paige nodded. "Like I told you, he's as nice as he looks, with the most spectacular manners you ever saw on a guy. Too spectacular, really."

"I saw your stepsister, too," Judy said. "Is she going to try to live up to you or are you going to try to live her down?"

"Judy!" Paige said, looking around nervously. "Please be careful what you say."

"Don't Judy me," her friend said curtly. "I'm not quoting anybody. That's my own unprejudiced opinion. But if I ever saw trouble in a pink skirt, it's that one!"

She and Judy parted after the first class and the day moved speedily on. In a way Paige wished the classes were meeting for whole periods. Instead, they had only enough time in each room to meet the teacher, get the book requirements, and write down one assignment. It was amazing that in a school that big, she managed to see Katie Summer every time she changed classes.

After English, Katie was in the hall surrounded by a group of boys. She was laughing and sparkling the way she always was when she was the center of attention.

Outside of geology, Katie was leaning against the wall with her bright blonde head bent over the school map in a tall boy's notebook. As she passed, Paige realized the boy was Ted Warner, one of the guys in her class. Molly Cavannah had been going steady with Ted when school let out in the spring. Every time Paige saw Katie she was with one boy or more.

Maybe Katie didn't believe in talking to other girls!

Maybe other girls didn't want to talk to her.

Yet, as many times as she saw Katie, she never saw Tuck once. She really watched for him, too. It had to be tough to start as a senior in a new school!

Katie was glad the classes met only for a few minutes. She was too excited to sit still any longer at one time. She couldn't wait to write Jill about the boys in Philadelphia. They were all so *tall*, and friendly, too. Mrs. Foster had certainly been right about her accent. Every single one of them had noticed it, and most of them had commented on it. But they were always compliments. One guy had even said he could listen to her talk forever.

She couldn't say so much for the girls. When she tried to catch their eyes and smile, they looked away. The only girl who had been halfway nice to her was Jayne Singleton, who wasn't her sort of girl at all. Jayne was too . . . maybe acid was the word, and she was almost rude. Southern girls were taught to be less overt.

Katie watched the girls leave class in little groups of two and three, and she ached with envy. Were they naturally unfriendly, or had Paige already poisoned their minds against her?

CHAPTER 14

Paige waited for the others by the front door of school after her last class. It had been stupid not to make some arrangement about meeting when classes were over. With such a mob of kids pouring out, she would be lucky not to miss them. She had waited only a few minutes when she realized she had worried in vain. She heard Katie's appealing laugh down the hall and saw her coming with Tuck on one side and Ted Warner on the other. Her blonde hair shining in the sun, she waved cheerily at Paige as she approached.

Hypocrite! Paige whispered to herself.

"I'm so excited I could die!" Katie cried. "Swim team tryouts are this very afternoon. Tuck's going to run me home for my suit, and back I come. Isn't that the most exciting thing? I'm so nervous I'm just trembling."

Ted Warner mumbled something and went on

out the door. Tuck stood silent, then turned to Paige. "Any place you need to go, Paige?"

"Tuck, you didn't hear me!" Katie said. "I've got to get home and back."

"I heard you, Katie," he said. "But you are *not* the only fish in this pond."

"That's okay," Paige told him. "I'm ready to go home."

"Okay, that's fine then," Tuck said. "Come on, Katie, let's go."

Katie was audibly suffering in the back seat as Tuck wound out of the parking lot. "Can't you hurry?" she begged. "How can I make the team if I'm late?"

"Simmer down," Tuck told her. "Running into a half dozen cars is no way to make time."

"That's all we need," Katie said, slumping down angrily in the back seat. "*Another* wet blanket in this family!" All the way home she tapped one foot impatiently against the back of Paige's seat.

When Tuck pulled up into the driveway, Paige saw Jake working at the back of the yard. He stood up and smiled at them. Katie was out of the car in a flash. She waved gaily at Jake, blew him a kiss, then shot inside. Paige followed, leaving Tuck at the wheel. Paige had barely greeted Miss Aggie before Katie came pounding back down the stairs and out the door again.

"What was that about?" Miss Aggie asked, staring after her.

"Tryouts for the swim team," Paige explained.

Miss Aggie grunted. "Looked more like practice for the hundred yard dash."

When Paige giggled, Miss Aggie asked, "School okay? Want a sandwich and some milk?"

"Maybe when Tuck gets back from delivering Katie to school," Paige said. "Thanks anyway."

Before Paige got to the stairs Jake rapped at the back door. "She's gone," Miss Aggie told him.

"Paige is gone?" he asked. "I wanted to talk to Paige."

Paige turned reluctantly and went back to the door. "Hey," he said. "Has being a junior already given you a big head? You must have a *minute* to rap with an old friend."

Paige caught her breath with difficulty. "Maybe a minute," she told him, letting herself out the door. "What's on your mind?"

When he looked at her in that intent way, she couldn't meet his gaze. Why did she have to keep seeing him holding Katie close with their lips joined? She wanted to get away from him, far away so he couldn't compare her with Katie.

"Do I have to have something on my mind for us to talk? I just wondered what was going on. Tuck and Katie flying in and out like that."

Paige let her breath out slowly. Okay, he wanted to talk about Katie. Why hadn't he said so? "Katie had to get her stuff and get back for swim team tryouts."

"Ah," he said, nodding. "That's right. She mentioned trying out."

Paige nodded, still standing.

"We could sit on the steps a minute," he suggested. "I'm way overdue for a break."

Paige felt panicky. She couldn't let herself in

for this. He would sit there and talk about Katie and she would want to die. "I'm overdue to get out of these first-day school clothes," she told him. "Tuck will be along soon. He'll take a break with you."

As she turned, he caught her arm, sending that awful shiver up her spine. "Paige," he said gently. "What's going on?"

She shook her head. "I don't know what you mean."

"Of course you do. I haven't seen you for ten minutes since you came back from Atlanta."

She was never going to get out of this unless she could lighten it up somehow. "Look who's complaining!" she said brightly. "You have all the company anybody needs at this house."

"Oh, you mean Katie," he said thoughtfully. "It's different with Katie Summer, Paige. You're my *friend*. Katie's . . ." he paused and shrugged, "like nobody I've ever known . . . or should know, probably."

Paige turned away. "Look, I've gotta run! See you around."

She knew he was still frowning after her as she closed the door, but she didn't look back.

Upstairs in her room she tightened her fists against her eyes, willing herself not to cry. The room smelled funny, of cologne and fingernail polish remover. Her unmade bed looked different and worse with Katie's side of the room in perfect order. Even after dumping her clothes on the bed and putting on her running suit, she still didn't feel like herself. It was as if a stranger were in her skin, a hideous stranger, jealous and mean and angry.

She couldn't hear anything from downstairs. Tuck had been gone a long time.

She tiptoed down the stairs and was going into the study, the one place that was really hers, when Tuck ran through the hall. Even in the dim light he looked different, his face swollen and his jacket stained.

"Tuck," she cried. "What in the world?"

He turned away angrily. "Nothing, let me alone."

"Hey!" she said, catching him by the arm. "Come off it. Something happened, and it looks like it hurts."

He pulled his arm away and glared at her. "So I was in a fight just now. I don't want to talk about it."

She had never seen Tuck like this. With his balled fists at his side, his stance was as hostile as his words.

"Have it your own way," she told him, "but I wouldn't have asked if I didn't care."

He stared at her, then shook his head. "Okay, Paige," he said, lowering his voice a little. "You got anything upstairs for this cut on my face? I'd just as soon not advertise what happened."

"Second shelf in the bathroom," she told him. "And if you want the bloodstains to come out of that jacket, soak it in cold water before you put it in the hamper."

Her words made him angry all over again. "Regular little mother, aren't you, Paige? Well, get off it. I already have more mothers than I need. Boy, was I set up for that bunch of guys! I no more walked into school this morning than they started baiting me, hooting at my manners, my clothes, the way I talk. Mom set me up for this with her steady nagging about being a 'gentleman' instead of a roughneck. How would she have liked seeing me battling two guys who think I belong in a museum?"

"Tuck," Paige cried. "That's not fair. You can't blame your mom — "

"I can, and I do," he broke in, turning to take the stairs two at a time.

As Paige looked after him in silence, the back door banged, and the little girls thundered through the hall and past her on their way upstairs.

"Quietly!" Virginia Mae called after them. "Tuck? Paige?"

"Here I am, Mom," Paige said. "Tuck's up in his room."

Paige followed Virginia Mae into the living room where her stepmother collapsed in a chair. "I can't believe the energy those girls have. They wore me to a frazzle just coming home from school. Jake saw me and he's going to pick Katie up from swim team tryouts. What a relief! I may *never* get out of this chair." She looked up at Paige. "How was your first day as a junior?"

"Fast," Paige told her, stricken by hearing that Jake had gone to pick up Katie. "But okay," she added hastily when Virginia Mae looked up with concern.

* * *

When Katie found Jake instead of Tuck waiting outside the gym door, she hardly believed her luck. All the way home he listened to her tell all about the tryouts.

"You're going to be really tied up between swim practice and your studies," he said.

"It's not *that* big a deal," she laughed.

"That school is known as one of the toughest around," he warned.

She didn't want to talk about school or even the swim team any longer. Why didn't he talk about *them*? Or had he had his final say? She hoped they might drive around a little, maybe have a Coke to celebrate, but he took her straight home.

She hoped he might kiss her again the way he had before. Instead, he pressed her hand tight and let her out of the car. He looked at her for a moment and then he mumbled, "I'll see you."

But at least she had made the team!

She fairly danced into the house. "I made it, Miss Aggie," she announced. "Where is everybody?"

"In here," her mother called out to her. "Come and tell us your news!"

The room looked warmly cozy with the drapes shutting out the light and a single lamp by her mother's chair. Paige sat stiffly across from her new mother.

"Did you make the team?" Virginia Mae asked eagerly.

Katie nodded, remembering. "It was such wonderful fun. I was scared to death. I haven't practiced since we left home. There was a big gallery of people watching, as many guys as girls." She hadn't meant to brag, but she couldn't hold it back. "When they announced my name as a team member, the guys all clapped."

"Congratulations, Katie Summer," her mother said. "I'm proud of you. How about the rest of school?"

"Super," she said. "I couldn't believe it. Such great guys!"

Virginia Mae sighed. "Katie!" she protested. "I was asking about school. You know, teachers, classes, courses!"

Paige didn't turn away quick enough to hide her amused smile. It enraged Katie. Who did Paige think she was to smirk in her particularly annoying way? Wasn't it bad enough that Paige had probably turned the girls at school against her without giving Katie a chance on her own?

Katie ran her fingers through her hair and started out the door. "Do I look like a book-worm?" she asked, looking directly at Paige. "Aren't there more important things in life? Like people?"

Then she left swiftly before her mother had a chance to answer her.

CHAPTER 15

As the days passed Paige felt bleak and listless. The last time she had felt that way was when she went to camp, and it rained. Then she had known she was homesick. That was ridiculous. How could you be homesick in your own home? The answer was easy . . . spelled K-A-T-I-E.

In the old days her father had brought home briefs from the office. After supper he did his work by the fire in the living room with Scarlett dozing on the rug at his feet. When Paige and Megan finished their homework, the three of them talked, or played games, or struggled with the jigsaw puzzle on the coffee table until Megan's bedtime.

School nights were not the same anymore. Paige's father never brought his work home anymore. Either he and Virginia Mae went out for the evening, or the two of them sat by the fire. When Virginia Mae played the piano for him the way Paige used to do, Paige felt bleakly jealous in spite of how much she liked Virginia Mae.

Doing her homework was the worst. She had always studied flat on her stomach in bed, with her favorite classical radio station humming companionably behind her. Katie studied sitting up in bed against a pile of pillows. Katie not only liked a completely different kind of music, she liked it played at top volume.

I have nothing against rock music, Paige told herself crossly. It's when it is banging inside my head that I can't stand it!

During that first week the teachers took it easy with assignments. The second week Mr. Bertram assigned three full chapters of geology with the hint of a pop test in the same breath. Right after supper that night Paige went upstairs, half-heartedly straightened her bed, and flopped on it to tackle the reading. Before she was halfway through the first chapter, Katie Summer came in, turned her radio on at top volume, and began to study, too.

Since Bill Whitman and Virginia Mae were out at a law association dinner, Paige considered taking her book downstairs. But her father had spoken to her quietly already about what he called her "rudeness" to Katie. She didn't want to have him do that again. She gritted her teeth and concentrated on the page again. It didn't work. Not only was she reading like a third grader, one careful sentence at a time, but she had to read most of the paragraphs over a couple of times to get any sense out of them. This was crazy. Just when Paige thought she couldn't stand it another minute, Katie Summer got up and left the room.

Paige waited, thinking Katie would be right back. When a long time passed with Katie still gone, Paige turned her rock music down and went back to reading.

That peaceful silence lasted about two minutes. Katie returned, walked across the room glaring, and turned the music back up, looking at Paige defiantly.

Paige looked back at her, desperate enough to ask her a favor. Katie smiled with a "What are you going to do about it?" look.

Paige drew a deep breath, gathered up her books, turned off her own radio, and walked out.

Paige stood indecisive in the downstairs hall. She couldn't go to class without getting the chapters read. And she certainly couldn't go through the rest of high school without doing any homework.

The kitchen was too public, anyone could come in and out of there for a cold drink or a cookie or whatever. The living room might work this one night but the problem would remain. The only other downstairs room was the playroom at the end of the hall which had been Megan's and Mary Emily's special territory since the wedding, but they didn't study there at night!

Paige cleaned off the end of the table, pulled up a chair, and moved Megan's teddy bear lamp over from a bookcase at the end of the sofa. She missed her radio for the first few minutes until she got interested in the text. She took better notes than she had ever been able to lying down.

123

At the end of the first chapter, she took a cold apple from the refrigerator and tackled chapter two with a feeling of real achievement.

Feeling victorious, Katie watched Paige leave. That would teach her that she couldn't pick on somebody without expecting them to hit back. She opened her book again and looked at it blindly. School was going to be fun. The guys were wonderful. The girls probably would be, too, if they gave her a chance. She was absolutely certain Paige had talked to them about her. Why else did they look as if she were a freak of some kind and turn away when she approached? Except Jayne, of course. Maybe she *should* cultivate Jayne a little. She sure didn't want to go all year without anyone to hang around with!

Tuck startled her by appearing in the open doorway. "What do you think you're doing?" he asked, shouting.

"Studying, what do you think?"

He crossed the room and turned the radio down. "Nobody could possibly study with all that noise."

Katie leaned over and turned it back up. "I obviously can."

He looked at her a moment before turning on his heel and leaving the room. She had barely settled when he was back, handing her a set of earphones. "Now," he said. "Use those if you must go deaf. Other people have rights, too."

Katie stared at Tuck. They had always been close . . . able to talk. And here he was acting as if they were enemies, talking to her in that bitter, disapproving tone.

It was Paige's doing.

Paige had not only turned all the girls at school against her, she had made Katie's own brother hate her.

"*Other people*," she said bitterly, fighting a sudden rush of tears behind her eyes. "Like I didn't know who those *other* people are. Like I didn't know Paige came around whining to you, turning my own brother — "

"Paige?" he interrupted her. "I haven't even seen Paige since supper."

"Don't give me that," Katie said. "I know she put you up to this."

He shook his head. "Nobody had to put me up to anything. I've been sitting back there in my room with my ears covered, trying to do my calculus. I don't know how Paige or the little kids stand it at this end of the hall. "Hey," he paused. "Where is Paige anyway?"

"I don't know, and I don't care," Katie said, grabbing the earphones and plugging them into the radio. "And get out of my room, and don't come back in without knocking."

"Don't worry," Tuck said. "I've got enough problems of my own. I don't need yours!"

"What kind of problems do *you* have?" Katie asked. "Mom loves you and Paige loves you and Bill thinks you're great."

"Yeah," Tuck said angrily, "all I have to do is get used to fighting the guys at school."

Katie looked at Tuck with surprise. "What do you mean fighting?"

"I mean fighting, fists, feet, words. They seem to think I'm a wimp, a ridiculous guy. They hate the way I talk and dress and breathe."

"Tuck," Katie called out, as he turned away. "I'm sorry. Really."

When he left and shut the door behind him, Katie turned over and cried into her pillow for a long time. Nothing seemed to be working out, and she yearned to be back home in Atlanta.

Paige lost all track of time. She finished reading all three chapters, went back over her notes, and was checking out a couple of things she had written down without really understanding them. Scarlett began to bark when she was halfway down the last page. "Okay, okay," she whispered aloud to herself. As soon as she finished that page, she would walk the dog and be through for the night.

Instead, the door opened. Her father and Virginia Mae were standing against the light from the hall, staring down at her.

"What are you doing here?" her father asked abruptly.

"Studying geology." Without thinking she rose to her feet, as if she had been caught doing something she shouldn't.

"I thought you always studied in your room?" Virginia Mae asked, her voice giving away her concern.

Paige gripped the book to her chest. "I usually do but this geology is so heavy duty . . ."

Virginia Mae looked at Paige's pale face. "I

think you and Paige should talk alone," she told her husband and left the room.

With his wife gone, Paige's father closed the door. "That explanation doesn't convince me. I've seen you in action with Katie, and I don't like what's going on. I don't like the way you look at her. I don't like the way you treat her." His voice rose steadily as he spoke. "I'd like a straight answer. What made you come down here?"

Paige looked back at him steadily. He wasn't really asking. He only wanted her to admit to something he imagined. Didn't he even care about *her* pain?

"I'm waiting, Paige," he said, his tone sharp with impatience.

She felt suddenly heavy with defeat. "Dad, you know how serious I am about school. You know how important I think it it to get good enough marks to be able to pick the college I want to go to — "

"Quit changing the subject," he said firmly.

"You asked me why I came down here," she wailed. "That's what I'm trying to tell you. I'm not used to studying in a room with someone else. Geology is hard for me. When I wasn't able to concentrate upstairs, I looked for a place where I could really get my work done. What's *wrong with that*?" Her voice shook with anger that she couldn't control.

He stood very still for a moment. "Wrong? The rudeness in your tone for one thing. But more important is the way you treat Katie. You've done nothing but make trouble for that kid ever since she came here. This has to stop, Paige. I don't mean I *want* it to stop, I mean it *has* to stop. This is a family. I don't intend to let you rip it apart with your stubbornness. Do you understand?"

No matter what happened he was determined to blame her. "I understand," she said quietly, "but I would like to study here when I'm having trouble concentrating."

He looked at her a long moment. "For study only, Paige, and only when absolutely necessary. You have to learn to get along with Katie."

Paige could tell he wasn't through, but Megan and Mary Emily came clattering down the hall. Then Virginia Mae was laughing with them in the kitchen. "Come on out with the rest of us."

Mr. Whitman didn't give Paige a chance to reply but turned and left, closing the door behind him. Paige gathered her books together, blinded by tears, and followed him into the kitchen.

That night Paige lay sleepless a long time after Katie finally turned out the light. How much of this trouble was really her own fault? She hadn't liked Katie from the first, but she had sincerely meant to try. Jake's attraction to Katie that very first day had made it impossible.

Losing Jake was bad enough. The slow painful way she was losing her father was even worse. But he was right. She never *had* used that impudent tone of voice to him before. But then, she had never had to before. She had always been able to be perfectly honest with him and know that whatever happened, he was on her side and would lean over backwards to see her side of things.

He wasn't that way any more. He had too many people to be loyal to all at once. She couldn't be honest with him at all any more.

And Katie? Katie had talked and joked over popcorn in the kitchen as if she had forgotten their fight over the music. But Katie hadn't forgotten. The minute the two of them were alone, she acted as if Paige were not even there. She didn't say a word or even look Paige's way once they were inside their room.

Paige shivered under her covers even though she knew the room was warm.

CHAPTER 16

Paige thought of the playroom under the stairs as her retreat. Even when Katie stayed after school for swim practice, Paige studied down there, where she was only a few steps from the kitchen in case she wanted a snack or a cold drink.

On Tuesday afternoon she was fixing herself a Coke right next to the kitchen phone when Jake called. He sounded rushed, but she figured he was just disappointed that she wasn't Katie.

"Have her call me when she comes, Paige? She has my number."

Paige wrote the note: "Katie . . . Call Jake," and pinned it to the family bulletin board. She sighed. She had never had Jake's number in the year she had known him. But then, unlike Katie, she had no reason to call him. She took her glass back into the playroom, wondering if she was ever going to get over hurting when she heard his voice. She hated herself for having so little pride that she still loved him.

It was impossible not to know when Katie came home. She was . . . in a word . . . loud. She was always either laughing or singing, or talking brightly with whoever was in the kitchen. Paige closed her mind to the extra noise and went on with her work.

She thought about Jake's call. She had been thinking about it off and on ever since it came. She had put up the note. The bulletin board was there for everybody to check. Theoretically Katie Summer could read. Why should she *tell* Katie?

Dinner went cheerfully with Mary Emily and Megan talking about campaigning for a friend who was running for class president. Katie, of course, had her usual triumphs to report, and Virginia Mae was excited about an exhibit she'd seen at the art museum. Katie didn't ask if she had any calls and Paige didn't volunteer anything. But Paige kept picturing the note on the board . . . and ignoring the picture.

A little after nine Paige smelled popcorn being made in the kitchen and heard the voices of her father and the kids in there. She was putting her work away to join them, when the door burst open. She looked up to see Katie in the doorway, scarlet with rage.

"*That*," Katie shouted, "was the meanest thing I've ever heard of in my whole life!"

Paige stared at her, too startled to realize what she was talking about for a moment.

131

"Mean, hateful, ugly, that's what you are," Katie went on. "Just because you don't have a guy, you take it out on me."

"Hey, hey," Paige's father called from the kitchen. "What's going on out there? What's all the racket about?"

Katie turned, her hands balled into fists and her eyes snapping with rage. Paige saw the whole family there behind her, watching the scene.

"It's about *her*," Katie said angrily. "Paige is just out to make trouble for me."

"Lower your voice and explain what you're talking about," her mother said with warning in her voice.

Katie was fighting tears. "There you go again," she told her mother. "You don't even know what I'm mad about and you are already sure that it's my fault. I'm not going to take that. I know whose fault it is. Go on, ask Paige if Jake didn't leave a call for me today!"

"Yes, he did," Paige said. "It's right there on the bulletin board."

"But you didn't *tell* me," Katie's voice was rising again. "You sat there all through dinner and never said a word. He called just now. Do you know what I missed? I could die! He and a bunch of his friends got together this evening. He wanted to take me along so I could meet them. He wanted to see if I'd feel comfortable with . . . Never mind that. Now I've missed that chance, and he thought I'd decided I didn't want to see him. She hates me. Paige hates me."

"Katie, please control yourself," her mother said.

"But, Mom, I missed a wonderful party," Katie wailed. "I heard music and people laughing behind Jake when he called. It isn't fair that I didn't get to go."

"Paige," her father said sternly. "Come in the kitchen. I think we need to talk this out."

Paige crossed the hall with a sense of dread. Tuck was tactfully giving his full attention to the Coke in his hand, but the younger girls were staring wide-eyed.

Virginia Mae startled Paige by taking her hand. "Before we have that talk, Bill, let's check the bulletin board. Paige *said* she put the message up there."

"Oh, it's there all right," Katie said. "I saw it after Jake called. But she could have *told* me."

"That is unreasonable," her mother said firmly. "The bulletin board is there for messages. Paige isn't your social secretary. If you don't check for messages, you have no one to blame but yourself." She paused. "In fact, I think you owe Paige an apology."

"Apology!" Katie cried out. "For ruining my evening? For letting Jake think I didn't want to see him? She didn't forget, she deliberatcly didn't tell me." Katie wheeled and ran out of the room.

"Katie," her mother called after her. The only reply was the sound of the door slamming upstairs.

Paige stood silent, feeling guilty and exposed. "I am sorry," she said. "Maybe I should have told her."

"You certainly *should* have told Katie, and you know it, Paige," her father said angrily. "I thought I made myself clear to you on behavior like this."

When Paige said nothing, he would have begun again, but Virginia Mae touched his arm. "Let's forget it for now, Bill," she said quietly with a glance at the wide-eyed younger girls.

Upstairs, Katie pressed her cool hands against her hot cheeks. Paige hadn't forgotten that message. She might get away with that innocent act with some people, but not with her. If she said she had forgotten about the call that was outright lying, and Paige had managed to get her into trouble with her mother again. She was in for another lecture the first chance her mother got.

"I hate that girl," Katie said aloud miserably. She glared around the room, wishing she had some sneaky way to get even with Paige. But Paige's trick had been too slick. Anything she did now would only get her punished.

"That's okay," Katie said. "I'm keeping score. One of these days I'll get the chance to get even and then some."

The first school dance was held the following Friday night. Katie studied the poster carefully. Nobody was supposed to come with a date and no one but registered students would be admitted. That let Jake out. But even if he wasn't there, she could have fun. She'd hardly had a chance to dress up since they moved.

When Katie mentioned the dance at home, Tuck just shook his head. "No way, not for me."

His mother looked at him in surprise. "Tuck, you've always liked dances."

"I don't anymore," he said without looking at her.

Mr. Whitman studied him for a moment. "What if I ask you, as a favor? Virginia Mae and I plan to be out that night, and you'd be the only one here to drive the girls."

What had come over Tuck? His face darkened the way it did when he was angry, and he didn't answer at once. Katie saw her mother's anger rising, too. "Tuck," Virginia Mae said firmly, leaning toward him. "Bill asked you a question."

Tuck's voice betrayed his anger. "I was trying to think of some way to keep from being trapped into it," he told her. "I don't want to go, but it looks like I'm caught. How about I drop them there and pick them up when it's over?"

Mr. Whitman looked ready to agree to this, but Katie's mother was not about to give in. "It won't hurt you to try *one* dance at this school. You'll be here a whole year, you know."

Tuck looked at her. "Is that an order?"

Her blue eyes snapped. "It's an order, Tuck."

Paige said nothing. She hadn't planned to go, either, but now she didn't dare mention it.

Her father grinned at Megan and Mary Emily who were punching each other and giggling. "I'd say Miss Aggie will have her hands full with those two that night!"

By Friday night Katie was really excited. Would the guys who had been so nice to her at school turn out to be party types? She loved a

135

dance where everybody came without dates. Nobody could get mad if guys swarmed around her.

When Katie went upstairs to dress, Paige was not there. She had already showered, laid her outfit out on the bed, and gone to walk Scarlett. That was great. Katie could take a long leisurely shower using the bath gel that made her skin feel like satin.

When she undressed and went to the closet to hang up her school clothes, she squealed at the shock of something cold and squishy under her bare feet. "That slob!" she said, jumping back quickly. Paige had left a sopping wet bath towel right in front of the closet door.

Katie stared at the wet towel thoughtfully a minute. Then, picking it up gingerly between her thumb and one finger, she threw it on Paige's bed. Actually, she dropped it on the dark red pleated skirt Paige had laid out for the dance. But that was an *accident*, just like forgetting to tell Katie about Jake's call had been an accident!

Katie took her bath gel to the bathroom and sang as loudly as she could in the shower.

Paige heard Katie singing as she came upstairs. She peeled off her jeans and shirt and reached for the skirt she had laid out on the bed. For a minute she thought it was gone. Then, with sick horror, she saw the hem of it sticking out from under the wet towel. "I don't believe this!" she breathed.

She threw the towel across the room and lifted her skirt. It weighed about five wet pounds and the pleats were spread in the wet wool.

136

Paige dropped the skirt and held her breath. She wasn't going to scream. She wasn't going to make a scene the way Katie did. The towel she had thrown had hit the top of the dresser and spilled Katie's silly ruffled basket of perfume samples all over the dresser and into the top drawer, where Katie kept her fancy matched bra and panty sets.

Paige crossed the room in swift steps. She didn't move a thing, not even the towel. Impulsively, almost without thinking, she loosened the tops of about six of the perfume bottles so that they spilled onto the dresser and Katie's clothes. The smell almost made her sick as she pulled another skirt out of the closet, shook it, and started to put it on.

She wasn't quick enough. She was reaching for the zipper when Katie, her hair wadded into a towel, appeared in the door.

"What's that awful smell?" Katie asked. Then, seeing the wet towel draped over her perfume, she wailed. "Look what you've done!"

"I just tossed a towel," Paige began.

Katie flew out of control, crying helplessly as she tried to get the bottles sealed again. "You tossed a towel," she yelled. "A nasty wet towel *you'd* left on the floor. . . ."

"You *ruined* my wool skirt," Paige told her hotly.

At a giggle from the doorway, both girls wheeled. Megan and Mary Emily, in their matching nightgowns, were leaning against the door helpless with laughter.

"Get out of here!" Katie yelled. "What do you think you're doing?"

"Watching you fight!" Mary Emily said brightly.

"You're like Saturday morning cartoons, the way you yell at each other," Megan added.

"I don't yell," Paige said crossly.

"Smell this room!" Katie cried. "She deliberately spilled all my good perfume!"

"It stinks," Mary Emily said.

"The whole business of sharing a room with a pig stinks," Katie said. "And my beautiful underwear is soaked!"

"You two shouldn't even *try* to share the room," Megan said. "You should tie a rope right across the middle like the red flag in your closet. Then each of you would have half a room."

"Draw a line!" Mary Emily put in. "It could be the Mason-Dixon line with Katie getting the southern side."

"I told you to get out of here," Katie repeated, as Megan went into a fresh attack of giggles.

"Let me show you where to draw the Mason-Dixon line," Megan went on. "Right down the middle of the closet, right down the middle of the dresser . . ." She was dancing across the room with both arms straight out like a wooden puppet.

"Or one could take the top and the ceiling and the other have the bottom and the floor," Mary Emily put in brightly.

"When I say get out, I mean it," Katie said, shoving both girls toward the door. The girls giggled down the hall.

"A Mason-Dixon line!" Paige said with disgust. She sat studying the room without smiling.

"That was better than their last idea since neither of us can fly. . . . It isn't working, is it, Paige?" Katie asked quietly.

Paige shook her head. "Not only is it *not* working, but I'm *sick* of having everybody mad at me all the time."

"What about me?" Katie cried out. "Not everyone is exactly crazy about me."

The two girls were silent. Their anger and frustration and confusion filled the room.

"Well," Katie said, "they *are* married. So we *have* to live together. And it would be nice if we could bear it at least."

"I don't see how," Paige answered. "Do you?"

"Partly it's the matter of the way we keep our things," Katie said thoughtfully. "I'm neat and you're . . ."

"*And* the music," Paige added quickly.

"*And* the dirty tricks," Katie said angrily.

"*And* the dirty tricks," Paige said loudly.

"Didn't they draw up some kind of a compromise to settle the Mason-Dixon line?" Katie asked after a few moments.

"They had to or they wouldn't have drawn the line."

Paige sat on the bed, only to jump away quickly to get off the wet spot. "We only need to do three things: we divide the room with no trespassing, no loud music on either side, and no dirty tricks. I can't stand living with all this anger any longer."

"I don't exactly thrive on it," Katie said.

The girls looked at each other and then around the room. "Okay," Katie said, "it's a deal."

She held out her hand toward Paige. Paige stared at Katie's hand and then thrust hers into it. "It's a deal," she repeated.

They sat silently for a few moments and then Katie said, "I don't have any underwear, unless you want me to go to the dance smelling like a perfume counter."

Paige tugged her dresser drawer open. "Don't expect any neatly folded piles. Just fish around in that clutter until you find something that will work."

"Thanks," Katie said softly.

"You're welcome," Paige answered just as softly.

The dance was going strong when they arrived in the gym. The music was a five-piece combo with a wonderful drummer. Katie felt strangely shy walking in with Paige and Tuck. Almost at once she realized that Paige was really trying. For one thing, Paige introduced her to some of her girl friends, something she hadn't done before. They weren't all serious, unsmiling types as Katie had expected. Judy Belnap was darling and would have made a hit anywhere, even in Atlanta.

None of the girls was very friendly, but they weren't rude either. The minute Katie and Paige stood still, a tall, good-looking boy came over to ask Paige to dance.

"Alex Moore," Paige said smoothly, "I'd like you to meet my new family, Katie and Tuck

Guthrie. See you later, guys!" she said as she lifted her arms to Alex.

As Katie stared after them, Tuck rose and took her hand. "Come on, Katie, let's see how far we can get before some guy steals you. As long as I'm here, I might as well dance."

Katie watched Paige dancing with Alex. She was a smooth and very graceful dancer. Alex leaned toward her smiling and obviously having a good time. "Have I underestimated Paige?" she asked Tuck.

"It's been pretty mutual," he said.

She grinned at him. How lonely it had been without a girl friend. Was it possible that she and Paige could ever really be friends?

Suddenly Katie felt a tap on her arm. A pretty, dark-haired girl was standing next to her. "When you finish dancing with your cute brother with that cute accent, can I have the next one?"

Katie grinned and moved aside. "You can have him right now. I'll do fine on my own." Her eyes moved around the gym, looking for a guy to dance with. She held her breath when she focused on two boys leaning against the wall, staring at Tuck with apparent hate in their eyes.

Katie touched Tuck's arm and moved her head in the direction of the two menacing-looking boys. She felt the muscles of her brother's arm tighten under her fingers. "Tuck," she whispered, "I don't like the way they're looking at you."

Tuck shook her hand off his arm and took the pretty girl's hand. "Don't worry. I can take care of myself."

Katie hoped so.

CHAPTER 17

Even though the line across the room was invisible, it worked. Through the following days, Paige realized that her own untidiness was really not because she liked it that way but because she was usually thinking of something else. More than once when she stopped at the door to check, she saw that she had absent-mindedly done it again . . . dumped something in Katie's space.

Because Katie was equally careful to respect Paige's space, Paige was startled to come into the room and find a piece of paper on her bed. When she picked it up, she saw it was a colored ad for cosmetics torn out of a fashion magazine.

"This yours?" she asked Katie.

"Oh, that," Katie shook her head. "I tore it out for you. Look at that girl. She's almost your twin. Same face shape, same thick hair, same eyes, and slender neck."

"Gosh," Paige said, staring at the model. "I don't look a thing like that."

"Sure you do. Look." Katie caught Paige's long, dark hair and cupped it under at her shoulders. "Now look in the mirror. See the difference? You'll have to pretend you have on mascara to bring out your eyelashes and blush to accentuate your cheekbones."

Paige turned impulsively. "How can I imagine makeup when I've never tried it?"

Katie couldn't believe her. "It's so much fun to experiment with! Sit on the edge of your bed and hold still."

Katie was as proud as Paige was astonished by the change brought about by a little eyeliner, a blush across the cheeks, and a soft rose lip gloss. "But I wouldn't dare have my hair cut that short."

"Why not? Hair grows a half inch a month. You could let it grow back if you don't like it."

When Paige looked hesitant, Katie plumped down beside her. "Let's make an appointment. I'll go with you for courage. And while we're out, we can look at makeup."

"I have to think about it first," Paige told her. When Paige went to the bathroom to wash her face, she looked in the mirror a long time and lifted her hair the way Katie had. She decided to leave the makeup on.

Tuck was the first to notice.

Staring at her, Tuck said, "*Look* at you! You look great like that."

Her father glanced over and did a startled double take. "Paige, I can't believe you."

143

"She looks like a fashion model, all except for her hair," Megan said without looking up from her plate.

"The hair gets changed Saturday," Paige announced quietly. "Katie's going with me. And Dad, I may need some extra allowance for make-up."

Her father laughed. "Good as done. Just so you don't have to buy all new clothes to go with your new face."

"What a brilliant idea!" Katie said brightly.

They looked at each other shyly, unable to believe they might be friends.

The haircut was amazing. Paige found herself looking in every mirror she passed, unable to believe the colorful, stylish face that stared back was her own. She especially liked the warm rose of the lip gloss Katie had helped her pick out.

"I wish I had a shirt or something this same shade," she told Katie.

Katie giggled. "Remember what your father said?"

"He was only kidding," Paige assured her. "He's always asking me if I need anything."

Katie knelt in front of her sweater drawer and pulled out a shaker knit vest in almost the same shade of rose. "What you should do is get a rose and white striped shirt and wear this over it." She sat still a moment, her eyes wide. "Wow, what an idea. We could pick stuff out together. We'd have twice as many outfits if we could pool them."

"I think your style is a little dressier than

mine," Paige said slowly, not wanting to sound critical.

"Actually," Katie said, "my style's a little dressy for this school. I could tone it down a little, and you could jazz yours up, and we'd meet in the middle." She laughed. "If I felt underdressed, I could always hang on some ribbons and scarves and junk jewelry and feel like the same old Katie Summer."

Paige groaned. "I don't know why we're talking about buying clothes. We don't have room for what we have already. And all this summer stuff . . ." She stopped.

"What's the matter?" Katie asked.

Paige said, "You know those closets under the eaves in the attic?"

"I've never been in the attic," Katie told her.

Paige felt a wave of sudden pain. The last time she had been in the attic she had seen Katie and Jake in each other's arms, but she couldn't dwell on past unhappiness if this truce was going to hold. "Come on," she said, "let's go look!"

The built-in closets ran all along one side of the house. While all of them had things in them, none was full. When it only took a few minutes to empty the first closet, Paige suggested they go for two.

The attic was filled with old furniture, toys, old books, and dusty trunks. Katie, coming from a compact apartment, was fascinated by the profusion of things. She wandered around, touching an old velvet sofa and opening yellowing books. Finally, she stopped in front of a sheet-covered painting. She pulled off the white covering and caught her breath.

Looking at her with wide blue eyes and a heart-stopping smile was a young woman. A woman whose bright red hair caught the sunlight coming in the attic window. She was wearing a soft, gray dress that hung gracefully about her.

"Paige," Katie breathed softly. "She looks just like Megan."

"It's my mother."

Katie stepped back from the portrait. "But why is she hidden away up here?"

Paige put the sheet back over the painting. "She was hanging in the living room, but Dad didn't feel it was right, after he got married, to leave my mother's picture there. It really wouldn't make Virginia Mae feel very comfortable."

"I guess that's true," Katie said. "It just seems a shame . . ."

"It's okay," Paige said. "I don't need the picture to remember her."

They didn't mention the picture again but started going up and down the stairs, bringing up all the clothing they didn't need right at hand.

After they had the clothing carried up and put away, Katie plopped down on her bed. "That was a job."

"But look at our closet now!" Paige said. "I may even break down and press something once in a while . . . just to show off, you understand."

Katie laughed and rolled over. "Glory, it's nice not to be fighting all the time, Paige."

Paige nodded. "Big switch, massive change. Oh no!"

Katie reared up. "What's the matter?"

Paige laughed. "This all started with that rose lipstick and a shirt to match. I'm the kid who would always rather die than wear *any* shade of pink."

"But we both wore pink to Mom's wedding," Katie reminded her.

"That's what I mean. Big switch."

The entire house felt different during that truce. Even Binker, finally accustomed to her new space, ventured downstairs to sit in the sunny kitchen window and keep Miss Aggie company. It really seemed as if Paige's father's dream of their all becoming one big happy family was finally coming true.

Paige discovered that if she just accepted Katie for what she was, her stepsister wasn't that bad . . . annoying sometimes, but who wasn't?

Jake made the fatal difference.

The pain simply wouldn't go away. Paige never wakened in the morning without seeing Jake's face in her mind, hearing his voice, his laughter. She missed him, being close to him and talking with him as a friend, if that was all she would ever be to him.

With Katie staying at school every other afternoon for swim practice, Paige had the same opportunity she used to have to talk with Jake. She decided the mature thing to do was to go out and talk with him as she had in the old days. At least she could make an effort to renew their old friendship. She thought about this for a whole week before getting up the courage to do it.

147

Jake was obviously glad to see her. Paige glowed when Jake said, "You're looking great, Paige. Really staggering." He asked about school and her friends, especially Judy Belnap, who had been around the house enough that he felt that he knew her, too.

Then boom! He started talking about Katie Summer.

"What about Katie making the swim team!" he said to Paige. "I guess I hadn't realized how much that meant to her. But then, Katie's full of surprises." He leaned back, his expression thoughtful. "I've never met anyone like her before." He looked puzzled. "If anyone had told me I would be attracted to someone as different as Katie, I would have laughed them out of town. Do you know what I mean?"

Paige swallowed and nodded. "You *are* very different," she said, wishing her voice didn't sound so hollow.

He nodded and smiled. "Not only different from you and me, different from anybody! The way she smiles all the time, and her desire for fun. She never runs out of things to laugh about, and I never have the foggiest idea of what's going to come out of her mouth. She's like sunshine."

Paige wanted to escape. There was no graceful way. Jake's expression turned thoughtful again. "You wouldn't believe how hard I fight against *really* getting involved with her," he admitted. "There's every good reason why I should keep my distance . . . the biggest one being I've got a lot of hard years of work ahead of me and . . . I'm too old for her." His glance was searching Paige's face. "What do you think, Paige? *Am* I too old for her? Too serious?"

Paige didn't like his studying her like that, but he didn't look away. "Who am I to say?" she asked. "That's between you and her." She tried to say Katie's name, but it wouldn't come out.

"And there's the business of her at school . . ."

Paige frowned. "What does that mean?"

He shrugged. "She's just so beautiful, and vibrant, Paige. There must be a dozen guys at her school who are dying to go out with her. I don't want her missing out on fun because she likes me."

Why did every thing he say have to come out sounding like a question?

Paige pulled her sweater tighter and stirred in the direction of the back door. She couldn't take any more of this without crying or screaming. "I can't imagine Katie missing any fun," she said sarcastically.

His glance was penetrating. "That remark could be taken two ways." Then he smiled. "But I know what you mean."

Before he could start in again, Paige moved toward the house. "I better take off. It won't be much fun for me if I don't get my practicing done."

"Thanks for coming out, Paige," he said, his tone warm. "I miss our talks. Don't make it so long again, okay?"

She nodded and fled inside.

Jake stared after her. Why couldn't it be Paige he yearned after? Paige could live with who he was and where he was going. But Katie . . . ?

CHAPTER 18

Mike Lynch was leaning against the wall outside the locker room when Katie came out after swim team practice. Mike was not only the biggest guy on the team but also the fastest. She had yelled herself hoarse, along with the others, when he broke his own record in free style. And he was great looking, too, with a broad, playful grin and dark, matted hair, as curly as Tuck's.

"You sure made good time today," she told him, smiling.

"Lucky," he told her, grinning at her.

"Sure," she laughed. "Waiting for somebody?" She tried to remember who was still in there getting dressed.

"Not any more," he said, falling into step beside her. "How about a lift home?"

"That's *really* nice of you," she said, not bothering to conceal her surprise. "I'd love it."

Mike talked about the team and its chances in

the conference and told some funny stories about the other members of the team. When they reached the house, Katie asked him in for a Coke. He didn't stay long, but it was nice and loose to sit and laugh with him. She saw him to the door and as he got in the car, he called back, "Thanks, Katie. My treat next time."

His car hadn't made it to the corner before Jake came around the porch and stood looking at her.

"Hi," she said cheerily, running down to him.

"Who's that?"

"Mike Lynch. He's on the swim team," she told him.

"Something going between you two?"

"He offered me a ride home," Katie said, a little insulted by his tone.

"And you had to ask him in?"

"Listen, Jake," she said. Why did he have to make her feel guilty when she hadn't done anything wrong? "Was I supposed to be impolite after he brought me home? What do you want of me, anyway?"

Her words must have stung because he turned away quickly. "I want to know where I stand," he finally said, knowing how unreasonable he was being, and unable to stop himself.

"*You* wan't to know where *you* stand?" she asked. "What about me? I can't tell where you stand for two minutes running."

"Katie," he said, turning to her. "I shouldn't have jumped on you. If I knew where *I* stood, I'd tell you."

"What does that mean?"

He caught her hand in his, hard. "I want you, and I don't. I don't know."

The minute he touched her, her anger was gone. "Oh Jake," she said. "Don't worry about Mike. He's just . . . well, just a guy."

He took his hand from hers and started away. "There's no reason you shouldn't see all the guys you want. No reason at all, Katie. I'm sorry."

How much she wanted to run after him. Instead, she made herself go back inside with an awful hurt in her chest as she shut the door.

After her painful talk with Jake, Paige avoided seeing him when she came in after school. She wasn't going to lay herself open for another session like that. But not talking to him didn't help. She was still always conscious of him when he was there. Worse than that, she couldn't keep from thinking about him even when he wasn't.

The days got steadily shorter the way they always did in early fall. Paige's favorite time to practice her piano was late afternoon, when the little girls were off with friends and Katie was swimming. One day she had worked on a Chopin etude until she had it nearly note perfect. Virginia Mae came in, still with her trench coat on, and sat by Paige until she finished the selection.

"That was lovely," she said quietly. "You put such delicate feeling in your phrasing."

Before Paige could protest, Virginia Mae went on. "I was deliriously happy when I fell in love with your father. I was sure that I wouldn't need another wonderful thing as long as I lived. It never occurred to me that my marriage would bring me another daughter so much like me."

Paige flinched inside. If she only knew. But she didn't want her to know really. It was wonderful to be loved and praised even if she didn't deserve it. "I'm not that great," she protested.

"I'll stand by my opinion," Virginia Mae said. "I do think we're a lot alike, we like the same things, and we both are a little shy. I scared myself today. I signed up as guide at the art museum. I don't know *any* of those people."

Paige looked at her in astonishment. "That will change right away. Look how quickly we became friends."

Virginia Mae nodded. "They are all awfully kind. One of the women I met also loves music. She gave me tickets that she can't use to a coming concert at the museum."

"How wonderful," Paige said. "Those concerts are fabulous."

"That's what I've heard. But Bill has promised Tuck to go to a soccer game with him that night. Don't say yes unless you really want to, but would you like to go with me, Paige?"

"I would love it, Mom," Paige said, turning to give her a hug. "How super, how really super!"

Jake was waiting for Katie when she got home from swimming. She would have gone straight into the house if he hadn't called to her.

When she approached, he looked at her in that sober way. "I'm sorry, Katie," he said. "I made a jerk of myself yesterday. I'm being unreasonable. I know it."

She shrugged, not about to argue with that!

His eyes were intent on hers and a sudden smile touched his mouth. "I'm *really* sorry."

Before she could reply, he leaned and dropped a swift kiss on the cheek. "I love the fresh, cool way your skin smells after swimming."

Katie shook her head. "You're a weird guy, Jake. How can you prefer the smell of chlorine to good perfume?"

"On you, it's easy. Speaking of perfume and all things bright and feminine, I can't believe how fantastic Paige looks. I did a double-take when I saw her. Who would have guessed all that beauty was hidden in my old buddy?"

Let's not go overboard here, Katie thought. "Amazing what a little paint and powder will do."

"Come on, Katie," he laughed. "She practically sparkled when I told her how great she looked! You are a wonder."

"One of the seven of the world, at least!" Katie said, reaching up to touch his cheek. "See you!"

She wriggled her nose at him. "Studies and all that."

She knew he was still watching her, but she didn't look back. Studies and all that, my foot! If he thinks he can tell me off about Mike, give me a quick apology and a kiss, and then stand there and rave about Paige Whitman, he's dead wrong. Paige sparkle? That was ridiculous. She wouldn't sparkle if she glued sequins on her nose.

When Katie let herself in through the kitchen door, Tuck was reading at the table with a Coke beside him. "Hi!" he said, looking up. "How's our mermaid flipping along?"

She grinned at him. "A real splash! I stayed a little late to watch the speed trials. That Mike Lynch is a real hunk."

When he said nothing, she went on. "What a man! He's a senior, isn't he? In your class?"

He closed his book and rose. "Is he the one who drove you home yesterday?" he asked.

She looked at him, surprised. "I didn't see you."

"I saw you," he said.

"Then you must have known who he was."

"Okay, I knew. Katie, must you always have a big screaming fit over every good-looking guy that comes along?"

"But it's just harmless fun," she protested. "That's just the way I am."

His expression was amused. "You mean fickle and flirtatious, Katie?"

"Stop that," she said. "I like people, *all* people. If being upbeat and kidding and laughing a lot is flirtatious, then that's what I am. But I don't flirt any more with a good-looking guy than I do with Miss Aggie or the newsman on the corner. I just don't see any point in not enjoying every minute you live. Being stodgy doesn't make things better, it just makes them duller."

"Okay, Katie. Okay, I get the picture." Tuck said.

"I just get excited about lots of things . . . clothes and perfume and rock music and parties." Katie continued heatedly, ignoring Tuck. "I couldn't be down in the mouth all the time if I took lessons, Tuck, it's just not me. Mom jumps on me with that southern lady bit. That's fine for people it comes natural to. If I quit doing things on impulse, and smiling and laughing, I'd be the world's worst hypocrite . . . and miserable, too."

Tuck laughed. "Okay, Katie, you made your point. You're wild and crazy and fun. I'm just on edge."

"Forgiven . . . this time," she grinned at him. Poor Tuck. He was having the same problem she was having, only backwards. She didn't have any girl friends at school, only interested guys. He didn't have any guys to hang around with the way he had back in Atlanta, but he didn't have to take it out on her!

She was halfway through the hall when she heard Paige shout happily from the study. She stuck her head in to find her mother and Paige standing together, with Paige's arms around Virginia Mae.

"What's the high excitement?" Katie asked.

Paige was grinning from ear to ear. "Oh, Katie, it's so neat. Your mom has tickets to a concert and has asked me to go along with her."

Paige's words were almost like a slap. Her mom had tickets to a big fancy concert downtown and hadn't even thought about taking her? Katie struggled for words. "That's great," she finally said. "That's really great."

Her mother, sensing Katie's annoyance, frowned a little. "I know you don't care for classical music, Katie."

"I *said* it was great," Katie repeated, not caring how rude her tone was. She turned away from the door without giving her mother a chance to reply.

She walked up the stairs slowly. Inside the room she glared at Paige's messy bed and slipped off her jacket.

"Let's see!" she said angrily. "I see Jake in the yard and he makes a fool of himself, raving about what a knockout Paige is with her new look.

"I go into the kitchen and my brother calls me a flirt just because I mentioned another guy.

"I'm not even through the downstairs before my mother goes out of her way to let me know that she prefers my stepsister's company to mine.

"What is this truce anyway? A license to pick on Katie Summer? Three strikes in just about that many minutes is about as bad as life can get!"

CHAPTER 19

Katie was quick to learn how much worse things could get. When her homeroom teacher handed her a printed notice to report to the assistant principal's office for a conference, she didn't think much about it. When she got down to the office, three other kids were already waiting their turn ahead of her. When none of them talked to each other but just sat staring at the floor or their laps, she began to feel edgy. By the time she was admitted to Mrs. Foster's private office, she felt fluttery.

Mrs. Foster was wearing a different shade of gray wool with a pale violet scarf. Her expression showed more concern than it had the first time they met.

"I'm not going to pretend I'm not disappointed, Katie," she said. "I am. All of us on the committee are. The fact is that your scores simply are not adequate for the level you are on. Unless you can pull your grades up very fast, we have no choice but to put you down a level."

"Put me down?" Katie echoed, unable to believe what she was hearing. Didn't Mrs. Foster realize what an embarrassment this would be to her mother? Didn't she realize that only now was Katie finding some girls in her group who could get past her accent. "Do I have to tell my mother?" she asked desperately.

Mrs. Foster hesitated. "Usually we like to have parents involved in a problem like this, but this is really a *very* early warning. We will definitely have to talk to her if things don't straighten out in a couple of weeks."

Then she smiled. "Other than that, I have great reports on you. The teachers like your sunny disposition. The swim coach thinks you are a very promising athlete. I'd hate to see anything change that."

"Two weeks?" Katie asked.

Mrs. Foster nodded. "I'll be rooting for you."

Paige was practicing her piano when Katie let herself into the house. Katie went quietly upstairs and rapped at Tuck's door. "Do you have a minute to talk to me?" she asked.

He made a face at the wads of discarded note paper all over the floor around his desk. "Why not? I'm sure not getting anything done here."

She sat on the edge of his bed. "What is all that stuff?"

"Calculus," he said. "This is one tough school in case you hadn't noticed. In more ways than one! What's your problem?"

"The same," she told him. "I had a conference

today with the assistant principal. She has given me two weeks to get my grades up or be put down a level."

He whistled softly. "Mom and Bill sure aren't going to take to that."

"It can't happen!" Katie told him. "Somehow I've got to keep it from happening."

He shook his head. "I've watched you run for Party Girl of the Western World ever since you came up here, but it never occurred to me that you weren't making your grades. I can't believe that anybody as competitive as you has let yourself fall behind."

"Don't lecture me! I need help. And you know I've never been a big studier, even back in Atlanta. That's Paige's thing."

He looked at her and shook his head. "I wish you'd quit trying to put so much distance between yourself and Paige. There's room for both of you in this world."

"Tell Paige that," she told him.

"Paige knows that," he said. "I've seen her grit her teeth more than once to keep this truce going. But Paige owes you one. She's been a knockout since you gave her the short course in her new look. You gave her a hand at your thing, let her give you a hand in hers. She's a good student. People like that have learned how to work effectively, and you're a quick learner."

"What if she turns me down? She spends so much time back in that little hole of hers, she could always say she didn't have time for anyone else's studies."

"You'll never know without asking. And, Katie,

160

we're all in this together. Bill and I were talking . . ."

"So what did you and Bill decide?" Katie asked, warily.

"It wasn't deciding. We think you and Paige are naturals. You balance each other, or will when each of you quits trying to beat out the other one. But Paige has had all those teachers you're getting now. She knows what they expect. The worst she can do is turn you down."

She stared at him, measuring her chances of getting Paige to help. What he was really saying was that she needed someone to help her, someone older who had taken all those courses.

"Get onto it right away. I've got my *own* problems," Tuck said, remembering the insulting remarks tossed his way in school that day.

Halfway out of the door, Katie turned back. "Don't say anything to the parents about this. Or even to Paige."

Tuck didn't need to know she had a better idea for a tutor than Paige. Jake Carson. Jake was already out of high school. Mr. Whitman had said he was a brilliant student. She would talk to Jake. She wasn't even embarrassed at having to admit to Jake that she wasn't making the grade. She would tell him not to tell her parents and Paige. He would understand that if she fell behind, she had to make it up the way *she* wanted to.

He would help her. She just knew he would.

"Why shouldn't I mention it to Paige?" Tuck asked.

"I just want it that way. I want to handle it myself . . . alone."

He grinned. "You're a funny, proud person, Katie. I promise. And good luck."

Jake was in the back of the double garage repainting storm windows. Katie stood in the doorway deliberately shutting off the light so he would look up. He looked at her in that way that still melted her heart as if she were seeing him for the first time.

"Katie!" he said. Her name sounded different when he said it. Instead of answering, and without hesitating, she crossed to him and fitted herself against his chest, taking the chance that he would welcome her near him.

"Unfair," he said, holding his paint brush clear out at the side. "You're taking advantage of an innocent, helpless male."

"Yes!" she said. "Great, isn't it?"

"Let me clean myself off," he said, breathing in the delicate, flowery cologne she was wearing.

"No, Jake," she said swiftly. "First I need to tell you something."

She pulled a crate over and sat on it, looking up at him. "When I came here they put me in the honors level at school because Paige had always been there."

His glance became wary but he said nothing.

"I didn't think it was right at the time because I'm not the student Paige is. I also didn't know how much difference there was between the high school I went to and this one. I should have said something then, but I didn't because they told me right off that I couldn't compete on the swim team unless I was in honors."

"They're stiff about that," he said. "Always have been."

"I'm not making it, Jake. They've given me two weeks to bring my grades up, or I'll be put down a level."

Jake's expression was genuinely surprised. "Katie," he said softly, "you can't let that happen."

"I know it. I talked to Tuck. He suggested I try to find a tutor who had done all my courses to help me catch up." She stopped, waiting.

He frowned. "Are you asking me if I know a tutor to help you?"

She shook her head and then smiled at him. "Jake, I'm asking if *you'll* be my tutor and help me."

"I can't deal with this and paint at the same time." He set the brush down and wiped his hands thoughtfully with an oiled rag. "What will your folks say about this?"

"They aren't going to know about it."

"Wait a minute!" he said firmly. "You can't lie to them. That will just make things worse."

"This isn't lying, Jake. I have a problem. I want to cope with it independently, as a grown-up. I can't deal with the embarrassment of the whole family being in on it. If you want to be paid . . ."

He knelt in front of her. "Katie. There's nothing I'd rather do than help you any way I can. I don't want money. But are you sure this is the right way?"

"It's only a few weeks," she reminded him. "We couldn't do it here, but the weather's still nice. We

163

could meet in the park and study in your car." She looked at him beseechingly.

He blew his breath out slowly, thinking. Then he shook his head, "I don't know, Katie. I'm awfully busy, and I've never tutored anyone. You can find someone better than me."

"I'd rather have you than anyone in the world, if you'd do it," she said earnestly.

He almost took her face in his hands before he remembered how strongly they smelled of turpentine. She leaned toward him and pressed her cheek against his. "I'll never forget you did this for me," she whispered.

"I won't let you," he said, smiling slightly. "When do you want to start?"

"Tomorrow if it's okay with you. You could pick me up after school."

"I'm not sure this is the way this thing should be handled, but okay. You're hard to resist, and I do want to help you."

I'm getting more involved with her than I should, Jake thought. But she is so irresistible.

CHAPTER 20

Student Council had let out early for a change. Paige and Judy were still in the hall when Mrs. Foster came out of the principal's office.

"Paige," she said in a delighted tone. "I haven't seen you to talk to. I hope you're having a good year." She frowned. "We are all in hopes that Katie is going to be able to settle down and catch up with her group. The thought of having to put her back into a lower level is really distasteful to all of us on the committee. She *wants* to succeed so much, and she really is a charming and beautiful young girl."

With a pat on Paige's shoulder she was off down the hall. Judy stared at Paige open-mouthed. "Was she telling you that Katie is on probation?"

Paige stared after her. "She couldn't mean anything else. But I know Katie hasn't said anything at home."

Judy whistled softly. "If your dad is like mine about grades, that would be some bombshell for you to drop at home, and I *bet* she wants to get those grades up. She loves all the attention she gets out there in her bathing suit."

Paige shrugged. "I don't dare be the one who drops that bit of information. Katie and I have both been trying to get along better, and while it's not always easy, so far it's working. After the way it was before this truce, Dad would land on me like a brick for telling something like this that was really Katie's business."

"Even if it's true?" Judy asked.

Paige nodded. "He's tougher since he has extra kids. Tougher and harder to explain things to."

Privately, Paige didn't think the truce was holding together as well as she had told Judy. Katie's open resentment over Virginia Mae inviting Paige to go to the concert, instead of asking Katie, still rankled. It wasn't fair for Katie to make up to Paige's dad the way she did and then resent it because Paige and her stepmother were friends.

But Katie wasn't winning on all fronts anymore anyway. Jake had stopped coming around in the afternoon the way he used to. To Paige that meant he wasn't seeing Katie. There had been a time when she would have died if she thought Jake had another girl. Now she couldn't be happier than if he found somebody besides Katie Summer.

But Paige missed seeing him.

When Katie first got on the swim team, she had gone to practice every other day. Lately she was gone every single afternoon. Since the room was always empty, Paige went back to her old habit of studying up in her room. She still liked to read lying on her stomach in bed.

Binker had snuggled in beside her for a while, then become bored. She gave a big spring and jumped up onto the dresser, landing on the edge of Katie's perfume basket.

"Not that again," Paige laughed, getting up to set the bottles upright. Binker, her head arched, was watching something in the street below. When Paige looked down, she saw Katie Summer coming out of the park across the street. As Paige watched, Katie looked both ways, then ran across the street toward the house.

Where had she been? She wouldn't have come that way from swim practice. One of the other swimmers always dropped her off.

Paige was still stroking Binker and staring absently out the window, when she saw a car pull out of the park drive and make a left turn down the block. She couldn't believe her eyes. Jake. That was Jake's car. He had driven from the same part of the park that Katie had walked out of. Why were they sneaking around like that? And why was Jake meeting her in the park and not even bringing her home?

She gripped the top of the dresser hard to control the wave of fury and pain that swept over her. She had been wrong about Jake having another girl. He was just sneaking around with Katie, so that nobody would know what they were up to. They were together! Jake and Katie.

She caught a deep breath and took her work

downstairs to the playroom while Katie was still in the kitchen laughing with Miss Aggie.

Paige spent the next hour trying to get herself under control. She hadn't realized how much it had mattered to her to think that Jake was losing interest in Katie. Why *should* it matter? He wasn't going to be any more interested in *her* just because he lost interest in Katie.

I'm so jealous of her, Paige thought. She's prettier than I am. We can wear the very same clothes, but she looks lively and colorful in them, while I only look dark and plain. She can wrap any man alive around her finger.

And even Mrs. Foster, who had always been Paige's friend, had said Katie was such a "charming and beautiful girl."

Katie might be charming and beautiful, but she was also a sneak who was fooling everybody in the whole world except Paige herself.

When her father called her to dinner Paige rose slowly, feeling wooden and dead. Lasagna was one of Paige's favorite meals, but that night it might as well have been cardboard. Paige toyed with her food and watched Katie from the corner of her eye. She was laughing and sparkling and being charming and entertaining.

"Do you know who I ran into in the hall today? Your friend, Paige, that nice Alex Moore. Jayne Singleton tells me he's the best student in the junior class." She laughed. "I told him I'd stand real close to him and hope some of it would rub off on me."

Something broke inside Paige.

168

She and Alex had always been good friends. She knew Alex, how shy he was, how easily embarrassed. He must have died to have been seen in the hall with Katie bubbling and prattling at him like that. But Paige really knew he had probably loved it . . . and had felt about Katie as he had never felt about her.

"Alex Moore?" her father looked over at Paige. "Don't I know that name?"

Paige nodded. "We've been in school together all the way through. He gave that talk you thought was so great at junior high graduation. He's in a lot of my classes, and we're on student council together."

"He's real attractive," Katie said softly, and smiled. "Not as gorgeous as Jake of course, but close."

Enough. The end. Katie deserved to be shot down, Paige thought.

"Which reminds me," Paige said calmly, slowly. "Mrs. Foster stopped me in the hall after student council today. Katie, she had *such* nice things to say about you. She said she thought you were a *charming*, beautiful young girl, and that the whole committee was *hoping* you would get your grades up so you won't have to be dropped to the next level."

Katie turned white. Tuck drew his breath in so hard that Paige could hear it, but Paige never took her eyes from Katie's face.

"Katie," her mother said in an amazed tone. "Are you having trouble with your grades at school? Is that what Paige means?"

Katie shot Paige a look filled with hate, then

169

she smiled at her mother. "I *did* get off to a slow start and Mrs. Foster talked to me about it. But don't worry, Mom, I've been working on it. I'm getting extra tutoring every afternoon that I'm not in swim practice. I would have told you, but I wanted to handle it by myself and not worry you."

"That's fine, Katie," Paige's father said. "I admire that. As long as you are getting the problem fixed."

"Oh, I am," Katie said brightly. "I was with my tutor this afternoon."

She looked at Paige, her glance defiant.

I'll take that dare, Paige told herself.

"With Jake Carson in the park?" Paige asked, her tone as innocent as she could make it. "What were you studying?"

Katie leaped to her feet. "You've been spying on me, that's what you've been doing. I wouldn't be surprised if you checked up with Mrs. Foster to see how I was doing because you were so jealous of the fun I've been having.

"Yes, I've been spending the afternoons with Jake in the park, and he's been helping me with my work. It was Tuck's suggestion that I get someone who knew the subjects to help me. I chose Jake instead of you for good reasons. He's not out to get me like you are. You're a sneak, Paige Whitman, a jealous, spying sneak, and I hope you're happy with what you've done."

Before she had finished, Katie had begun to cry helplessly. She threw her napkin on the table and ran from the room sobbing.

Her mother rose to go after Katie, then turned

to stare at Paige. "I can't believe this, Paige. How can you *treat* her like that?

"Look at what Katie has gone through! She's only fifteen, Paige, yet she cheerfully left her friends and her school to come up here and become a part of a new family. And what does she get for her pains? Coldness and spite. Anyone can fall behind in classes. Not everyone would have the spunk to try to catch up on her own. I'm proud of her, Paige, and I'm ashamed of you. You're not the girl I thought you were if you can treat Katie like that!" Virginia Mae whirled and left the room, but not before Paige saw tears of anger shining on her cheeks.

"Dad," Paige began. "She doesn't understand . . ."

"She understands all right, Paige," he broke in angrily. "We all understand. We have seen you do everything in your power to make Katie miserable in her own home. Virginia Mae put it better than I could. You have treated her too cruelly to be believed. Maybe Katie's right. Maybe jealousy *is* behind your actions. But whatever the cause, Paige, you're through making life miserable for Katie and the rest of us. If you took one honest look at yourself, I think you would hate what you saw!"

Paige felt herself shudder with shock. She had never burst into tears so swiftly and painfully. Deep racking sobs shook her entire body. Her father simply ignored her. When she covered her eyes with her napkin, he leaned across the table and pulled it away. "You're through hiding, Paige, behind emotional outbursts, insincere

171

apologies, and those endless explanations. Things are going to change."

Katie ran to the bathroom upstairs and locked the door behind her. She stood a long time leaning on the sink fighting for control of her tears. When they finally stopped, she rinsed her face over and over with cold water.

Finally rage replaced her self-pity. How could she have been so slow to figure out what was behind all of Paige's meanness?

Paige was crazy about Jake. That was at the bottom of everything. She had been crazy about him even before Katie had arrived. Now Paige couldn't deal with the relationship her stepsister had with Jake.

Katie stared at herself in the mirror a long time. "All right for you, Paige Whitman," she said out loud. "You with your put-on innocence. Now that I know what's going on, it will be easier. I'm *not* going to be thrown off the swim team. I'm *not* going to give up Jake Carson. In fact, I am going to keep Jake and flaunt him in your face every chance I get from now on. And that's not all. I'll make you pay for this evening somehow . . . just wait and see."

Katie left the bathroom smiling, ready to face Paige and whatever happened next.

Since no one thinks Paige can do anything right, she decides to do something really *wrong. Read Stepsisters #2,* THE SISTER TRAP.

172